I0537149

DAYDREAMS OF
SHANGHAI

DIMITRIY KAPLAN

Reviews for Dimitriy Kaplan's

DAYDREAMS OF SHANGHAI

"This is definitely a book!" *—lonely man*

"I've always thought about visiting China..." *—unknown*

"Hearing Kaplan's account of what happened really makes me want to reevaluate my life." *—former American co-worker in China*

"This is from the darkest and wickedest corners of my brother's memory chest. 'What happens in China- stays in China,' and this is my only chance to learn those secrets. However, it's no secret that I puked a few times when reading the first few chapters and our parents are so outraged that they stopped answering Dimitriy's calls. At this point, our only daydream is that he ends this nonsense nightmare by getting obsessed with a hobby more benign than sharing the traumas he survived in China." *—Concerned Sister*

"You're fucking sick." *—Editor*

DAYDREAMS OF
SHANGHAI

DIMITRIY KAPLAN

Dimitriy Kaplan Publishing
Miami Beach, Florida

ISBN-10: 0692842233

ISBN-13: 978-0692842232

ACKNOWLEDGEMENTS

Thank you to everyone who has assisted in the publication and launch of "Daydreams of Shanghai":

MARIA DE LOS ANGELES

EUGENE KAPLAN
NADINE KAPLAN
ANASTASIYA LYSENKO
CAIWEN LI

DAVID RIOS
MICHAEL BRIGGS
SERGE TYURIN
JAMES HARGETT
WILLIAM ROSSI
EDMOND AUYOUNG

DAYDREAMS OF SHANGHAI

DIMITRIY KAPLAN

Dimitriy Kaplan, who was born in Kiev and raised in New York, spent three years living in China between 2013 and 2016. During that time, he worked, for two years, as a university lecturer within Hainan Province, teaching courses in Western Culture and Oral English. His travels in China included over 17 cities in which Kaplan either lived or journeyed to, communicating with locals and studying Chinese culture by getting as close to living it as possible. He hasn't croaked yet but is patiently waiting to achieve post-mortem fame.

CONTENTS

PREFACE

While spending three years living, working, and traveling in China, I began brainstorming the creation of this novel. After jotting down many notes and repeatedly considering a multitude of absurd ideas, I realized I had more than enough to create *Daydreams of Shanghai*. As a matter of fact, I realized I had enough material for ten comparable novels. The culmination of my experiences in China was injected into *Daydreams of Shanghai* to reveal to readers the intricate and scarcely examined culture of China. Chinese culture, stemming from thousands of years of history (as the Chinese love to mention) is of course much too complicated to sum up in one novel. However, I hoped that as you followed Ting and Harry's adventures, you would begin to understand the cognitive dissonance I encountered while comparing China as it is with the China I had previously known. Huge cultural variations, historical influences, and ongoing cultural revolutions jumped to the forefront of my attention, as they should to yours.

I also hoped to portray the steadily growing American expatriate subculture dwelling within Asian nations such as China.

The vessel through which I communicate these ideas is, understandably, relatively satirical and dark, with short spurts of hope. Many Americans who visit China never come close to seeing the underbelly of the cities, deep-rooted in a history most could never witness or fully comprehend. The only way to do so is to live and intermingle with the native community on all social levels and in their native languages. What you hopefully will find, by delving into this rabbit hole of brain-fucking trauma, is understanding. Read this book with the knowledge that most will never know China like this, with the knowledge that needed to be scraped out of a dark, Chinese alley at four in the morning to fill the pages of this book.

CHAPTER ONE

A single drop of sweat lingered on Ting's brow, clinging to it for dear life. She glanced at the clock on the lusterless, gray wall. The timepiece had been frozen at two o'clock for the past six months and not a single employee was tall enough to replace the battery. It seemed her long days at the Huangyan Cigarette factory were growing longer by the week. Lu TingTing was one of two thousand workers assigned to her division, responsible for pressing the button to insert filters into China's favorite cigarette, the Double Happy Good Smoke. Ting would often peek through the dirty industrial windows of the factory and let her daydreams dance upon the smog clouds. If she concentrated enough, it would seem as though she wasn't in the mill at all. Ting could remember the countless joyful days of her childhood- living at home and toiling away in her father's medicine shop, completing hundreds of hours of homework to support the fading idea of a prosperous future, and slowly, yet somehow unknowingly, dying of air pollution. Her past showed more promise than working for an inferior salary at a dead-end industrial job, but there was always a chance she would find a rich man to sweep her off her feet.

Ting's best friend, Xiao DanDan, was a dimwitted and confident young woman that concluded her studies just two years before Ting. Having a high school major of "English Economics" put her in a prime position to potentially lead the Button Pressing Division of the factory. Ting's English level had been developed through years of strenuous studies at her public school but was still far below DanDan's. She often reminisced about the days the two would share a lunch in the school canteen. Gazing at handsome boys on the school playground was one of their favorite pastimes. Ting preferred the boys with the baby-faced look and considered men with facial hair to be Neanderthal beasts. DanDan couldn't do without the "hidden money" style, and she would often describe, in detail, methods for spotting boys whose families had a hidden surplus of wealth. She planned to one day marry a wealthy bachelor and constantly dreamed of the ways she would test his love for her. She imagined staging her own kidnapping, as a test of her future husband's devotion. This trial would effortlessly reveal the ransom this make-believe man would pay to get her back, she thought. DanDan was a complicated woman with intricate insecurities and flaws that Ting often misunderstood but always accepted. DanDan reveled in her ability to exert authoritative and unspoken confidence stemming from seniority, but Ting also thrived on those opportunities to relieve herself of all personal responsibility and dignity.

In many ways, the two complimented each other, but Ting often longed for more. Living in the dusty and dimming city of Huangyan and working every day for a vanishing wage was a dependable, yet daunting, existence. Ting continued to look back on her satisfying past while neglecting the future. After all, changing the future required effort and education, or at the very least, beauty. Ting's mother often reminded her that to be successful you need to be born intelligent or beautiful, as simply working hard was not enough in a country of over one billion people. Intelligence was out of the question. Her mother and father were both considered to be the spiritual guides of their local village and were therefore shunned by Huangyan's well-educated social circles. They had long since begun utilizing dreadful natural remedies such as Hairy Wolf Ear, Red Rooster Blood, and Crying Baby Teeth as cures for the superstitions that their ancestors had simply fabricated many years before them. The business had, however, experienced a slight rough patch as many customers began to contract salmonella and experienced many problems regarding the maintenance of their children's dental records. Despite these hiccups, Mr. Lu quickly developed a close relationship with the local police and was able to keep his business afloat. This allowed him to maintain his comfortable lifestyle and continue experimentation with a variety of lesser-known tradition medicines. He imported many crates of armadillo scales that were said to cure a variety of ailments including crying in children, excessive nervousness, demonic possessions of women, and ogre sightings. His ability to maintain valuable relationships and obtain rare ingredients meant that business would remain steady and booming.

For Ting, beauty was also out of the question. She had the unfortunate luck of experiencing a "horrific accident" as a child, tanning at the city's lakeside for nearly four hours before local residents could awaken her from the afternoon slumber. Her skin was henceforth considered "charred" by the community, and she would never again be the fair-skinned beauty that locals had always admired her to be. During this old and treacherous period of Chinese history in 2016, white skin was deemed a godsend in a godless country and Ting would never again be able to reap the rewards of her fair complexion. This would instantly make finding a suitable mate nearly impossible, as her off-white skin tended to attract mere street merchants and day laborers.

The concept of a *caili* suddenly became a distant hope, as no man would offer a high bride-price to such a lowly and obviously sun-tanned woman. Regardless, the Lu family continued to live their day to day lives, saving every penny for old age and new children, while dreaming of becoming overnight millionaires. Ting long suspected that there was more to this existence, but for her, an alternate reality was as far out of grasp as antiperspirant or razorblades. Her plans to begin a new life laid dormant for the first couple of years at the factory until an unlikely series of events presented her with more options than she had ever considered possible. These rare opportunities showed Ting that in life, anything can happen if you study your craft and press factory buttons very well.

The work day began as usual, with the gossiping howls of Xiao DanDan.

"General Tsao is making an unannounced raid on the first floor this afternoon, nobody knows about it," DanDan remarked as she hung up her tattered smock.

"Doesn't that mean that we need to prepare the red gift envelopes and *real* cigarettes?"

"I've already asked Wang Ding to do it, there's nothing to worry about. Since last time, we've begun to work additional hours to prepare the gifts."

"What should I do to help?"

"Pretend to keep pressing the button, he won't know the difference," said DanDan, turning away with a careless smirk.

Unspoken Chinese customs typically allowed for the chief of police to secretly notify companies of future raids so that they could prepare in advance. Once the raids were conducted, the company manager would need to grease the pockets of the equality-driven communists to pay tribute for the heads-up. This way, the company could continue to make cheap cigarettes with tobacco that looked, smelled, felt, and tasted like a newspaper. The police chief could then continue to maintain the dignity and honor of the police force with a new car and flat screen television. This seemingly complicated process strengthened the harmony and interpersonal relationships among community members but confused Ting, who didn't understand why they couldn't simply sell real cigarettes and avoid all this trouble. She quickly changed the subject, as publicly appearing confused was certainly considered a greater embarrassment than quietly remaining an idiot.

Ting and DanDan's direct supervisor strolled into the room. He snapped out of his afternoon daydream only after a lowly employee had already concluded their first segment of speech. Mr. Peng was often late to work and trapped within his own imagination. His main hobbies included drinking fine Chinese teas and playing *majiang* every Saturday evening with his business associates.

Unfortunately, these activities were all that would interest him and evoke a human from his lackadaisical shell. Years earlier, Mr. Peng took comfort in his ability to work hard to get to the top, working his way up from interning at his father's cigarette company to finally managing employees within his father's cigarette company. However, after his promotion to floor supervisor, he and his wife had begun to experience marital problems. His evenings were spent working at the office until the late hours of the night. Hers were subsequently spent in the bed of another wealthy businessman. This strained the relationship, though it couldn't be broken. If the union were to be dissolved, the family's honor and dignity would become both destabilized and tainted.

"Hello, girls," exhaled Mr. Peng as he proceeded, like a flaccid luggage case on an airport conveyor belt, through the room and into the bathroom for a cigarette. As General Tsao arrived, a member of the factory's administrative team initiated the playing of the Chinese national anthem. Every employee stood firmly upright and stared patriotically into the vast abyss of the hazy sky. The General stepped out of his Mercedes, and his officers propped the door open around his deformed leg. He hobbled into the main office of the factory with a big and noisy announcement exclaiming that he had, in fact, arrived. His left boot was black and shined like a fresh baby seal, though his right boot was only loosely attached to the shriveled limb. The leg was an unavoidable monstrosity that would never be the same since the accident. General Tsao had often delighted in taking his and his mistress' family on weekend ski trips, alternating weeks between the two. This was until the day he was caught upside-down between the seat and the wretched armrest of the ski lift. His leg was severely injured as his fat stomach dragged downwards on the extremity. The General had henceforth outlawed the act of skiing within the perimeter of Huangyan, and those that spoke of the terrible incident were inevitably kidnapped and tortured. Perpetrators that promoted blasphemous rumors almost always vanished and reappeared on the CCTV network, publicly apologizing for their great mistakes and damages to the nation's honor.

Mr. Peng arranged for the most beautiful of the female factory workers to be dressed in gowns for the arrival of the General. The low-status workers scrambled away from the factory floor, like filthy cockroaches exposed to light. They rapidly retreated to their dormitories. Mr. Peng's chosen females made their way to the entrance of the factory and kindly greeted the General. A giant, shit-eating grin overcame his face. He immediately proceeded to enter the facility with both hands clamped around the buttocks of the two nearest workers. The General's hands pulsated as they squeezed the women's bottoms and his index fingers slowly wandered.

"Yes, yes. Excellent, Mr. Peng. It appears as though almost everything is in order. I assume you have filed the banking account verification paperwork and all associated receipts? It would be a shame to have overlooked such critical procedures."

"Of course, General," Mr. Peng replied, as he handed the General a bright-colored *hongbao*.

The envelope was thickened and worn from the red bills it concealed.

The General proceeded back to the main office and answered his cell phone, though it was never heard ringing. After his brief and hurried inspection, he dragged his deformity back into the Mercedes and lit a golden cigarette as the driver quickly sped away from the factory lot. The alert light was shut off, and workers began to emerge from their dormitories that were located on the top floor of the building. Each room was a single unit and housed about twelve workers. Bunk beds lined the walls, and only a faint beacon of light entered the single, frosted windows inside. Male workers typically enjoyed nine hours of off-time per day, four of which were spent gambling while the rest were spent either asleep or masturbating. Female employees enjoyed less uninterrupted time, as many were forced into prostitution to reconcile any differences between their underpaid salaries and those of their male counterparts.

"Fuck the General. The police have the easiest jobs in China, they just sit in the station until it's time to collect their bonuses," mumbled a worker as he exited the bathroom through a cloud of smoke.

"But if they did not receive their bonuses, how else would they avoid doing actual work?" replied another, giggling.

"What shall we eat for lunch?" asked the third.

"Check out the tits on Ning today," blurted the drooling fourth.

Meanwhile, activities were resuming on the main floor of the factory. Ting crawled out of the broom closet she often utilized as a hiding space to elude the General. He had taken a liking to her during his previous visit and was very fond of grabbing her plump buttocks as well. She began to shut down the mechanized filter-stuffing machines for lunch time. She noticed DanDan exchanging a few words with Zu Cheng, a lowly and rather disappointing worker who was known for sleeping over seven hours a night. It often seemed as though there was no end to her laziness. Cheng appeared to be in a state of shock, and a single tear clung to her eyelash for dear life. Her smock was ragged, and her shoes smelled of garlic. The unpleasant scent often went unnoticed by her co-workers, who also secreted a variety of repugnant odors. She frequently dined alone, or with a single companion, and worked quietly without partaking in the usual factory gossip. Cheng did not smoke cigarettes, and she did not drink, as doing so would certainly label her as a "masculine" disappointment. Any minuscule chance she may have had to find a spouse would have then immediately disintegrated. Cheng was usually quiet and reserved, but Ting noticed that on this particular day there was an apparent sadness within her.

"Hey Cheng, have you eaten?"

"I'll see you both at lunch," blurted DanDan as she made her escape from the obviously uncomfortable conversation.

"I don't feel well today. My heart is broken."

"What happened?"

"I've just received a letter from my parents, my *meimei* is in trouble."

"Oh, my Mao! What kind of trouble? Last you spoke of her she was finishing up primary school and was about to enter a top middle school. She was an excellent student!"

"She spotted an expensive car on the street and ran into traffic so that the vehicle could hit her. It was an honorable act, she was trying to earn money for our family."

"Surely there are other ways to make money," replied Ting.

"It was a Porsche," Cheng defensively added.

Ting was unaware that when Cheng's sister had leaped onto the street, the Porsche stopped short about five feet in front of her. This nearly foiled her plans, but the girl was unrelenting. She charged towards the car and proceeded to throw her body onto the windshield- as if beaching herself atop the vehicle was comparable to being hit by it. She soon realized that she hadn't created a realistic crash scene and proceeded to crack the windshield with the top of her head. She concluded that this act would surely give the appearance of a real collision. The driver immediately began to dial 110 for police assistance, and dashcam footage would later prove the girl to be a cheater and a fool.

"I understand. Family is crucial to living a happy life," sighed Ting.

Ting continued to walk through the factory floor, leaving Cheng to ponder her current situation in peace. She wondered how the world could be so complicated and how so many problems could arise from seemingly mild circumstances. Ting didn't fit in with her surroundings, and she felt as though she didn't fit in with her co-workers and friends anymore either. She was detached from their daily problems and complaints. Why did her friends always need to please everyone else? What did her skin color have to do with finding a husband and why did she need a man in the first place? Why did they have to pay the General every time he visited the factory and why must they allow the pillaging of their buttocks to appease him? She was trapped in a world of complex emotions when all she ever searched for was simplicity. She entered the cafeteria, looking for a secluded area to eat in peace.

Soon after, Mr. Peng crept into the cafeteria at a rapid pace, clenching a folded notepaper in his delicate hands. He gave it to Ting with a worried frown and scurried away before she could react. He would often undergo meticulous preparation to avoid experiencing even a potentially uncomfortable moment. Ting slowly unraveled the note, and her mouth dropped to her lap. The note read: "Your parents are dead."

Ting was shocked and terrified. She expelled wild, banshee-like cries and burst through the exit doors as if covered in flames. In that very moment, her life was over. Ting raced out of the factory. Warm tears streamed down her face and flew off the edges of her cheeks. She ran home to assess the damage and as soon as she stepped through the door, her panic was reaffirmed. Her grandparents were sitting at the kitchen table, calmly snacking and ingesting liquor to ease the pain. They asked her what she had done to cause the horrific car accident that had so violently killed her parents. Ting was heartbroken when she realized they considered the disaster her fault. After all, it was impossible for her to have caused a car accident. The truth was that the crash was caused by her mother's careless, erratic driving. Mrs. Lu had become obsessed with her new, knock-off yPhone and would never let a message go unanswered for longer than a minute. Every text she received while driving was a life or death situation for her passengers, and on this occasion, Mr. Lu paid the price.

Mrs. Lu was cruising through a busy intersection, giving her neighbor the update on the latest gossip in the *hutong*, when she was sent flying through the windshield. She desperately and successfully managed to post her reply while midair. She landed on a pile of broken steel rods and was killed instantly. The last words she had ever communicated to anyone were pure malarkey. Mr. Lu was too bulky a man to squeeze through the windshield and his heart simply imploded upon impact, weakened by years of enduring traditional Chinese medicines. Ting laid, wallowing in her bed for days before even considering returning to work. This event would have nearly traumatized her, had it not been for her toughened character and willpower. Her emotional pain was especially debilitating as Chinese women were commonly raised with an idea of complete dependence on their parents. As a child, Ting was often told to obey her mother's wisdom without question. If she walked the streets alone during the night, she would die. If Ting accepted a ride from a stranger, she would die. If she became ill and kept it secret from her mother, she would die. And if she kissed a boy before graduating high school, she would get syphilis, and then die. Ting began to come to terms with her parents' passing within several weeks and decided she needed to get back to work and resume her normal life. Working hard and strengthening her independence would be the only way for her to ever succeed in this dark, lonesome world.

CHAPTER TWO

Stepping off a plane and onto foreign land was always easier after a tranquilizer and about nine or ten glasses of airline wine. Woozy and red-nosed, Harry slithered to the arrival gate entrance and peered through a crowd of about two hundred people. They appeared to have all been somehow related. Harry's luggage was lost in transit, and he quickly gave up on trying to communicate with the airline staff. After searching throughout the arrivals hall for what seemed like hours, a white sign appeared amidst the foggy crowd. It read: Welcome Shanghai, Harry Lice.

"It's 'Harry Price.' Are you with the Happy Family English School?"

"Yes, I speak English. I am FengPu, I will take you to apartment now. You have

33

ponytail, like girl. You look so old! Do you have wife?"

"Nice to meet you. And no, man. My wife left me two months ago. Let's get out of here, I can't wait to get some sleep."

"Yes. Yes."

Harry hopped into the blue cab hammered and gazed at the lush and developing scenery of this wild, industrial country. Brand new skyscrapers paralleled those that were yet to be completed, shopping malls the size of stadiums glistened in the late-summer heat, and the smell of burnt barbecue traveled hundreds of feet from the grill and into the cab's broken window. The sights of Shanghai could almost make a person forget the massive income gap caused by the government's totalitarian regime, the effects of which were evidenced by the people residing on the outskirts of town. Some of the apartments were so tall and beautiful, he thought. Once the cab arrived at Harry's new place, he soon realized that his apartment was not.

The loft reeked of molding oil and dirty socks, but then again, so did Harry. The shower produced a single stream barely capable of bathing a housecat, but for Harry, it was enough. The windows were permanently locked shut, but the air outside was poisonous and polluted anyway. In lieu of a gas stove, there was a single electric hot plate. In lieu of an oven, there was a single cabinet filled with soiled old blankets. Lack of amenities aside, the neighborhood was beautiful, and the weather was stunning. Children frolicked in the community area, and elderly grandparents gathered to play cards and share the latest community gossip. FengPu had provided Harry with an outdated, but free, three-bedroom apartment. It was just outside the hustle and bustle of Shanghai. Harry marveled at the spaciousness of his new apartment. He peeked into the bedroom nearest the bathroom. This room would later serve as a makeshift cemetery for emptied and shattered liquor bottles.

Harry had never lived entirely on his own before, despite having traveled extensively throughout the states for various odd jobs and short-term contracts. Most of his time had been spent living with family members and acquaintances. These periods of time attached themselves to his memories and would remain engraved on them for the rest of his life. He remembered that as a child, his older brothers would sneak into his room in the middle of the night and, while he slept, would place his hand into a bowl of warm water. This caused Harry to unknowingly urinate in his bed. Practical jokes were rampant in the Price household and often prompted reciprocal reactions. Days later, Harry began to quietly pee onto his brother's beds, claiming that he had also placed their hands into bowls of warm water as they slept and that they had created the stains themselves. One day, Harry was able to put a heavy bucket of water above one of his brother's bedroom doors, and upon walking into the room, the bucket had fallen directly onto his head without tipping. The plastic cracked, and the container was deflected by his brother's hard skull. Cold water soaked everything in the room and destroyed the brother's valued keepsakes. Harry bolted from the scene, though he was later caught and beaten mercilessly for drenching his brother's pornography collection. These were the memories that Harry had kept throughout the years, though every one of his five brothers was now the owner of his own household and Harry was, in many ways, alone. Harry was exhausted and excited. At least now he was, in a way, home.

Markin Thomas was the manager of the Happy Family English School and arrived at

Harry's new apartment at about five o'clock. He wanted to personally welcome him to China. Markin was a Canadian expat that had been living in various cities throughout China for over ten years. His former girlfriend of five years broke his heart and emotionally crippled him when she suddenly decided to leave and marry a wealthy Chinese businessman. The gluttonous sloth that she had fallen for worked as an exporter in a city called Shenzhen. Soon after their marriage, the sloth initiated a multitude of ongoing affairs with much more trustworthy and beautiful women. Markin never returned to his former self after the experience and had since been feasting on the souls of young and innocent Chinese virgins. His entire demeanor was that of a parasitic nomad. Markin's head shined during the day and stuck out like a mushroom in the grass during the night. His breath smelled of cumin and liquor, and his left eye tended to wander. As the sun went down, the creeping glint in his eye began to grow. Markin wanted to show Harry what a typical night in China was like for the expat community. They headed down the stairs, bypassing a flock of elderly trash-hoarders coming home after a day of scavenging. Harry asked whether they'd be able to stop and pick up something to drink along the way.

"You know, I've always heard that Chinese history is really rich," Harry remarked.

"Yeah, unless you're poor."

Markin returned to the previous conversation, stating that drinking was the whole point of leaving the building in the first place and that they would be going to an outdoor barbecue that was just a few blocks away. He mentioned that things might be slow because it was a Monday night, but for foreign English teachers, Mondays and Tuesdays were days off. The area of the city that they lived in was far from downtown, but not quite at the outskirts that were so often littered with filthy farmers and peasants. At dusk, the streets resembled authentic Asia, filled with bright neon lights, smoky grills, outdoor seating, scantily-dressed women, and scattered beer bottles.

"This is the place. We can pick up some drinks here and just bring them to the barbecue," Markin shouted from the crosswalk.

"Do they have liquor?"

"They have all this weird shit, but it doesn't taste that bad, and it's cheap. I usually get a small bottle of *sanbianjiu*, the three-penis wine, it's like two dollars."

"I'm not drinking penis wine."

"Don't worry about it, all the locals drink it. It's basically brandy with dog, seal, and deer penis soaked into it. It sounds disgusting, but it's decent."

Markin entered the tiny convenience store first. He nodded to the clerk and frantically scrambled to paste his Chinese phrases together. The novelty of his white skin distracted from the fact that the actual meaning and syntax of his words would have classified him as a lunatic in any other social situation.

"I think the owner's name is Ip," he said, "I have no idea, though, he speaks with a dialect, so that's why I can't always understand him. Anyway, this is where they store the different liquors."

The three-penis wine was festering in a large vat that resembled an enormous urn. Adjacent to the barrel was a rice-wine that the Chinese called *baijiu*. This spirit was a potent concoction that was not for the faint of heart. A bottle of it could kill a small horse, and five bottles of it could possibly even kill Harry. Markin pointed at the container of the lethal liquor. It encapsulated a variety of herbs,

39

twigs, and nuts. He motioned for two flasks worth of the liquid. The owner, Ip, smiled as his three crooked teeth peeked over his dry, scaly lips. Ip slowly lifted a single disposable flask, made of thin and delicate glass. He managed to spill about three vials' worth of the liquor simply by tipping the container and attempting to open it. Markin held one of the flasks to his lips and drank from it, rapidly emptying the fragile, glass shell. He was hoping to give Harry a great first impression of China and show him that this was how real expats spent their time abroad. Harry stood silently, waiting for his flask to be filled. In the meantime, he reached into his cargo pocket and took a swig from his personal, steel flask. Harry looked around the shop, noticing all sorts of different snacks he had never seen before. A molding stench from one of the shelves crept into his nostrils, but he ignored it. The store itself appeared to be decades old, and a single bedroom could be seen, tucked away behind the front counter. The owner's children were scattered throughout the store and chasing after each other wildly. They stared at and mocked Markin and Harry every time they looped back around. Ip's wife was heard coughing as she conversed with the television in the mysterious back room. A cloud of smoke emerged from the door of the chamber and slowly dissipated into the narrow hallway. Harry turned back and considered the glass case built into the front counter. Dozens of cigarette packs were arranged within the dusty display. Nearly 50 brands were available for purchase. Prices ranged from 50 cents to 20 dollars per pack. Harry called for three boxes of the cheapest brand and immediately began to smoke within the store as Ip quietly giggled.

"Let's get the fuck out of here, this place is beat," said Markin as he slapped the exit door frame and walked out.

Harry strolled out of the shop, thanking Ip for his help. He avoiding stepping on the children that were now rolling on the ground in front of him.

"White ghouls," murmured Ip as he retreated into his rotten wicker chair and blacked out.

CHAPTER THREE

Ting was happy to be at work and her first day back on the job was like a breath of fresh air. Returning to work after the tragedy would strengthen her and keep her level-headed. However, at the end of the work day, she would be left to her own devices to keep from thinking of her parents. She walked into the main office on the production floor to clock in. There was a large flat screen TV hanging from the beat-up concrete wall. It was the most expensive electronic device that most of the employees had ever seen. Mr. Peng sat in the office, lazily watching the bright screen. It showed scenes from the United States and depicted massive protests occurring in cities like New York and Washington. Women protested for trivial rights that were completely out of reach in

43

towns like Huangyan. Ting found the sight comical. She watched as women dressed like vaginas held signs and shouted in front of New York's glorious subway platforms. The next reporter transitioned to a scene depicting a white police officer arresting a black man. The officer was beating him mercilessly to confiscate what appeared to be a dull, black pistol. The Chinese government loved promoting these scenes of anarchy and blatant disrespect that were rampant in "free" Western countries. Ting shook her head and let out a quiet giggle as she walked out of the office.

For female employees, quitting time at the factory meant moonlighting in the town's darker quarters. These sinister crevices were filled with deviants and seductresses. Ting was repulsed by the idea of selling her body for a few measly additions to her savings. Others simply couldn't see a difference between being paid for sex and being paid to work as a masseuse. Most nights, Ting snuck out of the dormitory and worked at the YanYan fish market to earn additional money and to give her co-workers the impression that she was a working girl just as they were. She would pull a rusty, old bicycle from a bush beside the factory and walk it to the main road before mounting it. This would prevent her co-workers and managers from hearing her leave the factory headed in the wrong direction.

On this particular evening, the road was covered in dust. These days, it seemed that everything that Ting touched was either rusted or blanketed in a layer of filth. She rode under the moonlight for forty minutes before pulling into a low-hanging, tarp-covered pavilion. She then tied her bike to a greasy pole as she had done every night before, but tonight felt different. Ting felt the wild commotion in the marketplace and watched as workers hurriedly loaded a large shipping vessel.

Lang was the manager of the fish market and was a stern, but tender man. He was often called "Captain" by the workers, but Ting affectionately referred to him as "uncle." This was a way of showing respect to an elder since he was not her uncle by blood.

His demeanor was that of a humble and modest man that had seen things most could never even imagine. Lang's eyes were a faded, rich brown and his face was weathered like a leather wallet that had been sat on for decades. He had spent 23 years on the sea, returning to land frequently, though only momentarily, to drop his anchor in a variety of young, beautiful, and naive women that resided at various ports. Lang's crew had a great respect for him that most sea captains and leaders would never match. They followed and obeyed him relentlessly and supported him almost blindly. His fairness and passion for integrity and justice made this easy for most. After years of living on the sea, drinking seahorse brandy, and capturing sharks to assist Huangyan in the production of their prized shark fin soup, Lang had become the victim of a terrible and horrific accident. During the ordeal, he lost both of his hands in a battle to escape a deadly shark's grasp. Despite his ability to outmaneuver the various venereal infections that had been hurled at him by hordes of eager, harbor women, he was unable to escape the clutches of an even more fearsome sea creature. After several more years leading the crew and managing operations from the ship's cabin, Lang settled down and began to live on the docks. He ran the fish market from late evening to early morning. The Captain trained his entire crew to hunt the vicious sharks and everyone gained from these profitable exploits.

"Uncle, I'm happy to see you, we had another run-in with General Tsao at the factory today. He is so disgusting. I wonder if that rotten old leg will ever fall off!"

"He is a complicated man and is often tortured by his own demons."

"What demons?"

Lang had much more to say of General Tsao, but this was neither the time nor the place to discuss such matters. Regardless, they were just a part of the past. If Ting had known that General Tsao was a longtime rival of Lang's and that Tsao was the real reason that the Captain had lost both of his hands, she would likely be unable to refrain from disrupting the harmony between the town leaders. Lang was but a boy when he first met General Tsao, known as Colonel Tsao at the time. The two met at the town's lakeside while fishing on a rare, sunny, blue-skied day. Young Lang's incredible knowledge of various shark species intrigued Tsao, and a deep friendship was formed. Several months later, the colonel was promoted to General Tsao and used his *guanxi* to acquire an apprenticeship for Lang abroad Huangyan's finest sea vessel, "The Plain Dumpling." Lang then proceeded to excel in his mastery of the seas and was promoted to the rank of Captain by age 24. It was then that Tsao returned to Lang, asking him to pay back the favor.

"Forget all that. Come, Ting, I want to show you something on the ship."

Lang helped her climb aboard the battle-scarred ship and, right away, remembered the day that Tsao boarded the ship in a similar fashion. It was the day that Lang was promoted to Captain.

"This is a great promotion for your future, Lang, I hope you know that. If your father could be here to see you, he would surely approve. I think the only thing that would make him happier was if you were also sailing for China's independence."

"What do you mean, Sir?"

"Nothing, I only mean that we need more prominent leaders and role models to further the interests of the party at home as well as on the seas. Taiwan is a part of the People's Republic of China and must not be neglected. What if the people of Taiwan do not experience the greatness of real community, Mao forbid. They need to support a government that provides for the people. They will receive food, water, clothing, and comradery. The estranged worker is no more!"

"General Tsao, I am not one for politics. I only want to sail."

"And you will sail, while furthering the interests of your nation, paying respect to our great leaders, and promoting the party along various locations at sea. You have been chosen to transport political advisors and government officials to the rebellious island, along with secret law enforcement that will operate more... discretely."

Knowing that a direct answer would break surface harmony and cause tension between the two, Lang responded in the best way that he knew how.

"I'm sorry, I don't think there will be room aboard the ship for any extra passengers."

"Lang, please don't be foolish. There is no other option."

"I'm sorry, if any other passengers are added, the weight of the ship may be too great. It could sink."

"Surely the ship can handle six or seven more passengers."

"I'm sorry, the ship does not have enough seats to accommodate any more passengers, how terrible it would be if they were forced to stand throughout the entire journey!"

"Lang, I do not want to ask again. If you are unable to accommodate me, conditions may become unsuitable for you."

Captain Lang became incredibly distraught by this fierce and direct order, given by a man that he had previously looked up to. The General was a leader that he had always viewed as a role model. It became evident that Tsao had fallen into a downward spiral of endless political black holes. Lang adhered to common Chinese customs to avoid future confrontation. He simply ignored the request completely, and his life proceeded as usual. At first, there appeared to be no change and business ran smoothly. Lang assumed that his utilization of deliberate ignorance had worked, as it often did. Days, weeks, and then months passed without any contact from the General, but within a few years, the effects of Lang's great mistake were revealed. General Tsao had sent the secret police to board the vessel while Lang slept on a cold November evening. Waiting several years allowed Tsao to remain anonymous in his actions and prevent any potential blame to befall him. He planned to teach Lang a lesson regarding the development of a strong allegiance to the party. The officers that boarded Lang's ship during the night were attempting to dismember each of Lang's index fingers. This was considered a shameful public symbol of treason and disobedience to the party. They proceeded to mutilate the Captain when, in the struggle, they accidentally severed his entire left hand. This grave error would portray the General in a negative light, as officers of such high-ranking were forbidden to make even the slightest mistakes. Unable to openly admit fault or reconcile the mishap, the officers proceeded to sever Lang's entire right hand as well. This would not only make the act appear intentional but would solidify the intense and ruthless nature of the General's rule.

Lang snapped out of his daydream, reminding himself that this was long in the past and that any further dwelling on those events was unnecessary. He glanced down at his prosthetic hands. One of them frequently shed black paint. The other was shaped like a long peg and occasionally wobbled. He continued to lead Ting into the cabin of the ship. Lang then pressed down on the latch of a small steel box with the tip of his dildo-shaped peg hand. Ting had never seen such treasures within such a seemingly small and inconspicuous box. Even the outside of the container had a certain sense of character, tattered from years of being handled by the Captain's stiff limbs. Ting stared in awe at the riches within the metal case. She knew that Lang was living comfortably, but he was a mysterious man, and she understood that there would never be just one person that could fully comprehend him.

"That is an entire sack filled with money. Are those all red bills?"

"These are my life savings. I am not an extravagant man, I have not spent everything I have earned over the years."

"What will you do with it all?"

"The question is, what will *you* do with it all?"

"What do you mean?"

"Ting, with my simple desires, there is more money here than I could ever spend in three lifetimes. Half of this money is for you. I want you to take it. The Plain Dumpling sets sail for Shanghai in the morning, I want you to take the money and stay in the engine room until the ship arrives in Shanghai Port."

"Shanghai? But why? How? Mr. Peng will notice I haven't reported for duty, he will report the absence to General Tsao."

"This web of corruption only applies to this damned, rotting town. You are a free woman, with the option to work anywhere you want. You cannot live life fearful that your reputation and future will be destroyed if you upset someone. Think of your parents, Mao bless them, they would want you to succeed if they were still alive."

"You're right. But how will I find work in Shanghai? Where would I live?"

"I have a distant cousin that is about your age, you will stay with her. She will assist you as you search for work. With your experience, you will make it."

"What if General Tsao comes looking for me at the factory again? He often searches for me during his inspections."

"That damned pervert! Don't worry anymore, Ting. I have lived a good and honorable life, but I'm not of much use here anymore. Soon I will handle General Tsao once and for all. Now please, prepare to depart in the morning. The ship will set sail at sunrise."

Ting immediately thought of DanDan. She would be leaving overnight to an entirely different city, far from the grasp of corrupted Huangyan and far from the embrace of her best friend. How would DanDan feel, finding out that Ting had suddenly disappeared? Ting wondered if she would feel abandoned, or whether she would feel happy for her. Ting looked back to Lang and decided that at this very moment, DanDan was not as important to her as a successful future. Captain Lang handed Ting a smaller burlap sack with several rolls of money inside, this would be more than enough to last her the first couple of months. The bag also contained a small, rusted case with "LANG" engraved onto it. He kissed her on the forehead as he slowly withdrew from the cabin and headed back to the market. She stared at him lovingly. When she opened the case, she found a small, folded note inside. She unraveled the letter and held it up to the window of the cabin, tilting the paper to catch the shine of the moonlight.

"I will miss you."

-Uncle Lang

CHAPTER FOUR

Markin pulled up a few chairs as he and Harry arrived at the barbecue. He suddenly gestured toward the owner as if to throw a friendly punch and startled him.

"This guy always gets me a good deal," Markin mentioned.

The barbecue hall consisted of an extensive, outdoor seating arrangement with nearly twenty wooden tables that were situated behind a bulky central grill. Harry sat down on a rattling plastic stool and mixed his two glass flasks together into one. Markin then introduced him to a circus-like arrangement of fellow teachers and Harry was told that they would become his new co-workers after the weekend. He pointed to Shaniya, introducing Harry to a particularly dreadful specimen of the local expat community. Shaniya, typically categorized by her peers as a grotesquely overweight troll, thrived in the homogenous society of China. Her breasts were incredibly voluptuous and rippled like two waterbeds. They sagged down to her belly button every time she stood and oscillated when she walked. Chinese males marveled at the sight of her portly figure, especially since they had grown accustomed to flat-chested Chinese women who spent the better portion of their early and elderly years dressed like toddlers. They considered her a rare treasure and made use of every opportunity to spend time with her. This was because the men did not need to feign interest in dating her and were not required to produce gifts to sleep with her. Shaniya felt empowered, she had always considered herself a feminist and took great pride in her sexual freedom. She successfully made the tedious task of courting women obsolete for her multiple boyfriends. Their only complaint was that Shaniya was rather domineering and very dissimilar to their previous girlfriends, who constantly simulated weakness and fragility to raise the confidence of the men. Shaniya reveled in the attention she received in China and planned to marry and eventually gain permanent residence.

A sharp finger dashed across Harry's face and directed his attention toward another soon-to-be co-worker. Harry was introduced to Jonathan, who shook hands like an empress and never lowered his chin.

"Welcome to China, Harry. Or is it Harold?"

"'Harry' is okay, man."

"You almost remind me of my Victorian literature professor from my senior year, though he often went on and on about the repercussions of contemporary idealism in a modern fascist world. Interesting how we all forget the basics of democracy until confronted by pseudo-communism. Luckily, you don't strike me as that the type of person to get into that during dinner."

"Jonathan, what the fuck are you talking about?" asked Dean.

Dean was a fellow teacher, hired by Markin just three months before Harry's arrival. His inability to seduce Chinese women within that period caused him to develop an abrasive irritability that his co-workers were then forced to endure. Harry ignored his blatant rudeness and quickly scanned the faces of the other guests.

"And what's your name?" he asked, peering across the table at a young, blonde woman. She was freckled and elegant. She spoke only when it was absolutely necessary, and an intelligent, contemplative look came over her face in moments of serious thought. After briefly observing her, Harry came to believe that she understood the power of not only words but of silence as well, and she utilized both carefully. She was beautiful, slender, and spoke near-fluent Chinese to efficiently order food for the entire table. She was almost a drunken mirage. Harry wondered how a seemingly normal, sophisticated woman could be found among this group of heathens.

"Hi, I'm Colleen. Let's take a shot of *baijiu*, these guys are a little too much to handle right now."

Harry smiled and eagerly abided. Waiters began to carefully arrange food on the table. Harry was hardly sober enough to remain on his stool, though he did his best to avoid displaying his drunkenness for all to see. He was a typically a wild, but generally harmless, drinker. He was not yet familiar with his new co-workers, though, and wanted to refrain from appearing reckless. A waiter returned with a case of 12 bottles, amounting to a total of six liters of beer. Another waitress rushed to the table, balancing three plates on her forearms. The table was soon covered in regional delicacies and exotic dishes. Stewed frog legs emitted steam that softly coated the nostrils while grilled chicken feet lurked in the darkness of the table's edge. Grilled eggplant, chicken skewers, inedible leaves, potato salad, fried cabbage, and bottles littered the table. Shaniya inhaled a few of the frog legs before compressing them with a glass of beer and expelling a wickedly haunting belch. Jonathan rolled his eyes, and YuPi sat confused.

YuPi was Jonathan's friend and private Chinese tutor, but no one cared about him. He was a quiet wallflower and often tagged along with Jonathan, hoping to gain an understanding of foreign culture, though it would probably never help him escape his uselessness.

"Hey, nice to meet you," said Ricardo, who was sitting out of sight of Harry and finally emerged to introduce himself.

Ricardo had been living in China for three years, and he had moved to Shanghai after completing a long stint in South Korea. He had endured 10 years there, surrounded by enough blaring Korean Pop to send any sane individual to the psych ward. Ricardo's original departure from his hometown in

Arizona was sparked by a heated clash with a former fiancé, during which two of his teeth were knocked loose by an alarm clock while he slept. The fiancé had become convinced that Ricardo was cheating on her since his cell phone was protected with an intricate security lock. This prevented her from gaining entry to the device's contents, and she immediately concluded that only "scumbag cheaters" needed security locks for their phones. After this incident, Ricardo moved to South Korea and quickly found work as an English instructor. He was heartbroken, but he was also surrounded by many beautiful girls. Seemingly every girl in South Korea was attractive, but they often appeared to be underage and struggled to keep their big, gorgeous eyes from rolling out of their skulls. Cheap cosmetic surgeries were rampant in the country and quickly mutilated the natural eyelids that were typically efficient at keeping the girls' optics in place. Within two years, Ricardo was engaged to a young Korean girl who was nearly two decades younger than he was. At 42, he was more proactive about finding a mate but not privy to modern Korean culture and unaware of the cosmetic trends presently affecting the country. Ricardo's heart was broken once again after taking the girl out to the seaside for a midday picnic. He was planning to spend a lovely afternoon there, when the sun, beating down in all its summer glory, melted the woman's plastic face clean off. She soon dissolved into the great abyss of the ocean and was never seen again.

Ricardo continued with a brief version of the usual pleasantries before offering Harry a shot. Harry had found himself nauseated and bloated after consuming the restaurant's unfamiliar snacks and quickly excused himself to use the restroom. He promised to drink with Ricardo when he returned.

"Alright man, you're probably going to end up hanging out with the Markin and Dean crew anyway," Ricardo murmured as Harry turned his back to walk towards the restroom.

Harry squared off with one of the filthy and vomit-stained urinals. The bathroom smelled like a portable toilet that had been left unattended in a humid, summer heat. He lost his balance while leaning forward and managed to crack one of the shoddy bathroom tiles with his forehead. Harry stumbled backward, urinating on his left shoe, and barely regained his balance after grabbing hold of one of the stall doors.

Harry's forehead soon revealed a thin gash and blood began to drip from the opening.

"Ah, fuck!"

He wiped the viscous red liquid from his face with his shirt and exhaled a sigh of relief. Harry's feet then lost traction and slowly slid as he struggled to maintain his footing. He grabbed at the stall door once more, swinging it open as it had not been locked by its occupant. Harry immediately slipped in his own puddle of urine and landed flat on his buttocks inside of the occupant's stall.

"Ah, fuck! Sorry... Do you speak English? Do you understand 'sorry'?"

The occupant of the bathroom stall froze. He sat silently, squatting while smoking a cigarette with his right hand and texting with his left. To allow a squeal of laughter to be released was to shame Harry, and would result in him losing face. The occupant held his breath to keep from bursting out in laughter, and though his body did not expel the laughter, it did expel seemingly everything else. Harry retreated to the bathroom sink to wash off his shoes and the back of his pants. He exited the bathroom and lit a stale, old cigarette as he leaned against a fence post, hidden from the view of his dinner party.

Harry was dehydrated, but he was still able to produce a single tear as he thought of his ex-wife. She left him only a couple of months prior to him arriving in China. In all truth, she was most likely the main reason he left America in the first place. His life was unstable and fuzzy with her and his habits eventually forced her out of the relationship. Harry worried that his attempts to mend the broken relationship would prove futile if he continued this dangerous lifestyle in China.

As Harry returned, meandering towards the group, he noticed Shaniya and Jonathan assisting Colleen into a blue cab. She had become ill and defecated in her pants after trying to take three shots of *baijiu* at once. She ended up falling asleep on the dinner table while the stench lingered in her vicinity. The cloud of feces that surrounded her nearly caused the table to vacate. It was soon decided that she would no longer be able to continue drinking. Dean and Ricardo were seemingly unaware of the situation unfolding and had lined up four shots of *baijiu* each. Still, no one cared about or even came close to acknowledging YuPi. Markin stared at Harry to capture his attention. He then mouthed "let's smoke." Markin was exhausted from unsuccessfully attempting to lure

Shaniya back to his apartment after only 30 minutes of dining beside her.

"We gotta get the hell out of here, this place is beat."

"Alright man, I'm cool with whatever. This whole barbecue place is kind of cool, China seems way different than I thought it'd be," replied Harry.

"Ricardo and Dean are probably down to go with us to the next spot, but we have to make sure Jonathan and that awkward freak YuPi don't come with us. Colleen's basically dead and Shaniya is gross anyway, so we don't need them to get laid."

"Ah man, maybe I should head home. I'm jet-lagged."

"Nah, you're ok. Let's get Dean and Ricardo."

After walking back over to the group, Markin shouted that it was time to pay and that the group would be hailing cabs and relocating to what they referred to as a "KTV." The karaoke TV bar was located nearer to the city center and the group would often frequent various KTVs weekly. Markin turned and scanned the area for a waitress. As the Foreign Teacher Manager, Markin held the highest salary and offered to pay, in full, by pompously tossing 30 dollars onto the dinner table. This amount exceeded the dinner bill by nearly ten dollars. Markin was aware that the waiters would soon chase after him to return the change, seeing as the act of tipping was not customary in China. The waiters scrambled to clean the bills quickly, noticing that they had accidentally been thrown into the warm vat of frog-leg stew.

Markin also announced that he had ordered bottle service and that the KTV room would have a private waiter ready to tend to every vice imaginable.

"Ok. Dean, Ricardo, Harry, and I are going to the KTV, so we'll catch you guys later."

"KTV? I don't want to sit in a dark room and sing," replied Shaniya.

"Ok, then we'll see you later. And there's alcohol there, so why wouldn't you go?"

"Well, I guess maybe they'll have some cute waiters there," she replied.

"Gentlemen, unfortunately, YuPi and I will not be able to accompany you tonight. We have already made plans to go on a double date with YuPi's classmates," said Jonathan.

"Literally no one gives a fuck," blurted Dean.

Markin was already hailing two cabs. When they arrived, Ricardo, Dean, and Harry piled into the first while Markin boarded the second. He claimed that he planned to pick up female pedestrians on the way to the KTV so it would be better if he rode alone. The journey from the outskirts of Shanghai to the inner city showed a gradual transformation from old to new. It was as though they were traveling through time, departing from the dilapidated communist-era, and arriving in a modern, capitalist, skyscraper-filled metropolis. The taxi driver waited several minutes before beginning to blatantly gaze at Ricardo, who was quietly sitting in the passenger's seat. The driver muttered a few incomprehensible sentences every time he turned to face the road again. After realizing that he was not being understood, he rubbed his fingers together, alluding to the fact that he was asking Ricardo about how much money he earned every month. This was typical small talk in China, though such questions were considered particularly rude in Western countries. Ricardo pretended that he could not understand the driver and the confused cabbie soon glued his eyes back onto the road.

Within 40 minutes of riding and falling in and out of consciousness, the group had arrived. Bright, neon lights crept through the windows of the blue cab. Ricardo, Dean, and Harry squinted to try to get a better look at the KTV entrance. The taxi driver was still shouting in an unintelligible language as Harry was nearly crushed by oncoming traffic. The traffic and tempo of the inner city were much faster than that of the suburban regions located just outside of the hustle and bustle of Shanghai. Merchants waved balloons and glow-in-the-dark toys while street vendors smacked and cut oozing pieces of grilled squid. A man sharply veered his bicycle away from Harry and Ricardo to avoid clipping them with the sack of tin cans that loosely dangled from his handlebars. Ricardo excitedly crossed the street, walking toward the green and pink neon as if he had somehow reenergized himself in the moldy seat of the cab. Dean fell over a trash can trying to walk towards the liquor store and upon rising, couldn't comprehend why he wasn't on the other side of the street yet. Harry walked into the liquor store, leaving Ricardo to communicate his way into the KTV without any pantomimic assistance. Harry pocketed another flask and dropped a ball of crumpled bills onto the clerk's counter. His knees became weak, and he crumbled, falling backward through a tall stack of water bottles. The owner of the store immediately ran around the edge of the counter to assess the damage. His mouth smiled while his eyes saddened and drooped. Harry stood up and arranged the packs of bottles into an acceptable formation before stumbling back out of the store.

Once Harry crossed the road and entered the KTV building, a group of provocatively dressed hostesses greeted him in the luxurious lobby. They pointed him in the direction of Dean and Ricardo, assuming that because he was white, he must have been there to meet them. Harry reached his hand into his pocket to check his phone and upon withdrawing it, dropped a small wad of red bills. Realizing that a guest with money had entered, the hostesses took Harry by the hand and excitedly led him into the room that Dean and Ricardo were occupying. They were already singing and spilling beer all over themselves. Markin arrived alone ten minutes later.

"Sorry I took so long, I was working on this girl but she was so traditional, she didn't want to come. I may have some girls coming in ten minutes, let's finish this bottle of dick wine."

Markin threw the bottle at the wall after finishing it, and Harry's vision soon grew cloudy. He attempted to maintain consciousness, but it was a hopeless effort. He was on the verge of blacking out.

The first morning in China was chaotic, and Harry remembered only bits and pieces of the long night before. He remembered the broken beer bottles that littered the floor of the KTV room. Harry could picture waiters bringing beer, case after case, with fruit snacks intricately arranged on large glass plates. He seemingly remembered Markin leaving the KTV room with one of the waitresses, gripping her tightly by the hand. The next memory he could recall was the group eating grilled meats around a small wooden table, just before Dean was involved in an altercation with the staff that left his nose swollen and bloodied. Harry also recollected hazy memories of hailing a taxi home and watching Ricardo cut his hand on the rusted edges of the community fence after returning.

The warm sun beat down on Harry's head as he laid in his sweat-soaked bed. He rolled over, and his overwhelmed body shook the ground as it thudded against the smooth, warm floor. When he stood, his eyes drifted and refocused as if trying to adjust to an entirely new environment. Sunlight entered his room and crept into his field of vision. It appeared skewed like he was looking at the light through the lens of a kaleidoscope. He peered out of the window and after wiping his eyes with an old, moist rag, noticed a group of about 30 elderly Chinese women practicing *taiji* with long plastic swords. The sound of the music coming from the window was off-key and disturbing.

Harry washed his hands in the shower's single stream and was ready to go on the hunt for his breakfast. Every shop within a mile presented a logo of a noodle bowl on the window, and every menu was sloppily pasted to the wall. Every dish looked the same and was labeled in Chinese. Harry's Chinese speaking level was nearly non-existent, and his Chinese reading level was probably about that of a lamebrained toad. He wobbled into a noodle shop and was awkwardly greeted by the bewildered owner.

"NI YAO CHI SHENME DONGXI?"

"What do you have, man?"

"NI…. YAO…. CHI…. SHENME?"

"Right, yeah I'll have one of those…"

Harry pointed to a picture of noodle soup posted on the tile wall. This dish would soon become his breakfast, lunch, and dinner in the following weeks. He gazed around the restaurant, and it appeared as though the walls were painted "dust." The tables were the diameter of a truck tire and were only about one centimeter thick. In place of chairs, there were plastic stools that hovered above the ground. Everything in the restaurant was rickety and worn beyond repair. Portraits of Mao Zedong were hanging from every nail in the wall. The paintings were ironically positioned over the kitchen, despite Mao having starved millions of people just several decades before. Like the stools, Harry was on the verge of collapsing at any moment. His breath smelled of liquor, and he was sweating profusely. The owner brought the bowl of noodles within two minutes. It was steaming hot and smelled of fresh garlic and beef broth. He stood over Harry, waiting to see his reaction to the noodles and genuinely interested in whether this white, foreign gargoyle would enjoy the dish. Harry looked down at the soup with his glassy eyes and sweaty, sagging brow, and immediately vomited into the bowl.

CHAPTER FIVE

Ting quickly scribbled her name on the "Request for Work Leave Form Request Form." As she handed the form to the administrator on the factory floor, she was handed back the "Work Leave Request Form." This would allow Ting to make a peaceful escape from the building without making a dramatic scene. She was notified that the paper would be filed within six weeks, at which point she would be able to begin her work leave. Discouraged, Ting trashed the form and stated that she would not need to take leave at that time and that would file the form later. She planned to depart from the factory regardless, but time was running out. It was nearly sunrise. Her absence would be noticed by her co-workers but was not likely to be investigated. Due to recent changes in business procedures, they were more likely assume that she had committed suicide by jumping from the factory roof rather than presuming she had quit. Monthly ramp-ups in state-mandated factory production increased the weekly hours that employees were asked to work without increasing their salaries. Employees always had the option to strike, but seldom did as thousands of other townsfolk were available to happily accept their jobs. These steady increases in production were aimed at providing a lower cost option for cigarettes and thus sought to fuel the tobacco economy. This was a logical business plan for both factory owners and government officials. Chinese smokers were abundant throughout the country, and most had grown to become reliant on tobacco since childhood. They were the addicted slaves that were targeted by these local governments, who sought to exploit and profit from their dependencies. The step-up in production would also increase profits earned by both the medical and pharmaceutical industries. This chain of events almost instantly led to a higher frequency of suicides within the Huangyan Cigarette Factory. Factory employees were unable to cope with the increased stress within the work environment.

They were also unable to quit their jobs for fear of dying as homeless paupers, thrown into stagnant ponds and forever forgotten. In response to this increasing trend, Mr. Peng ordered the installation of twine netting to connect the rooftops of buildings located on Double Happy Good Smoke property. This would prevent the possibility of suicide, or so he thought. Employees would often become caught in the netting while still attempting to leap in a desperate effort to end their lives. Often, they would not be discovered for weeks, thus starving to death. Those that were discovered were left for dead by fellow employees, trapped in the netting. This was so that their co-workers could avoid somehow being blamed for the incident. Some workers were more resilient than others and soon located flaws in the construction of this netting. Their exploitations of these flaws often meant that a disappearance of an employee implied that they would not be returning to work. Mr. Peng hired several groundskeepers to patrol the area like vultures waiting for the dead. Ting sometimes saw them casually carting around lifeless corpses, with limbs hanging from the corroded wheelbarrows.

Ting used this knowledge to make her departure as quiet and discrete as possible. When the sun rose, she retrieved her bicycle quickly and began riding back to the YanYan fish market. Ting pulled into the pavilion once more and left her bike leaning against one of the shaky walls. The ship's engine began to roar as she propped her backpack onto her shoulders and started to run towards the docks. Ting lunged onto the entrance ramp with a couple of minutes to spare, climbed the slippery steps, and turned to face the shore. Not only was this the first time she was going to leave Huangyan, but it was the first time she would see a towering metropolis like Shanghai. The young ship Captain sounded the horn, and though it projected a piercing war call, few seemed to acknowledge the noise. The ship engine roared once more, and The Plain Dumpling pulled forward sharply. Several passengers that had pulled out their flip phones to take photos from the deck's edge were thrown overboard and left to swim back to shore on their own accord. Just like that, Ting fled Huangyan without a word. The future was no longer bleak, her pockets were no longer empty.

She slept for an entire day aboard the ship, tucked away in the storage closet down the hall from the engine room. Ting hadn't slept so long in years. She ate from a plastic bag filled with junk food and other delicious treats from her hometown. The second day on the seas, Ting rested. She spread her body across the storage room floor covered in mop heads and dust pans. On the third day, Ting continued to fantasize about her new life. She imagined a tall, handsome young man sweeping her off her feet with a proper car, apartment, and income. They would have a small five-bedroom apartment in the center of Shanghai, with only one child, to keep from overpopulating China. They would most likely need to find private parking for their BMW, she thought. The man could certainly not come from a middle-class family, but she would settle for upper-middle class if he were a government employee. She imagined dining at a cafe and ignoring beggars as she sipped fine beverages.

"I'm wearing French perfume, you fool! Do not breathe on me or it will wear off," she said, trying her best to keep from giggling.

Ting had spent so many years in Huangyan, the small town was all she knew. She could hardly even muster the imagination to picture what else people in China's mega-cities may do. She draped one of the mops over her head, lifted a dustpan and motioned as if fanning herself, to create a cool, pleasant breeze.

"No, thank you. No more tea or sweets for me, I'm quite full," said Ting, gesturing to the broomstick.

The fifth day aboard the ship, she heard the engine quieting down. It was running idle for several minutes before being shut off completely. An hour later, a single crew member descended into the bottom level of the ship and opened the door of the storage closet. He was her only protector aboard the vessel, hired by Lang and burdened with the task of watching over her. Ting quickly jumped to her feet and after being notified that the ship had reached Shanghai Port, excitedly ascended to the deck of the ship. She reached into her pocket for her phone and realized that it was nowhere to be found. It was too late to run back down into the ship and spend time searching. She was forced to leave without it.

What Ting saw astounded her and left her breathless. The Shanghai skyline erupted out of the river's banks. Skyscrapers as tall as mountains hovered over thousands of people scurrying between them. The buildings emitted a myriad of colors and flashed in unison. They projected Shanghai's most beautiful and prominent celebrities, right in the heart of the city. Ting looked toward the sky and toward the depths of the city and as far as Huangyan was concerned, she would never look back. She exited the ship and began to make her way to the port's information booth. This was the location that Lang told her to visit immediately after arriving in Shanghai. His distant cousin, Lina, would be meeting Ting there. Lang described Lina in incredible and meticulous detail, from her slightly wavy jet-black hair that reached her elbows to her red, embroidered skirts that she would wear anytime she left home. She had a collection of them that could account for every single day of the week. Her arms were unusually thin, and the girl had a large birthmark on her left hand. She was a real gem, with big, beautiful, sparkling eyes that hid under her pink baseball cap. She often wore thick, black-framed glasses, though they did not retain any sort of lenses. Lina was beautiful and quiet, but she certainly wasn't shy. Lang warned Ting of drinking alcohol with her, as she often could not control herself under such conditions and would wander the city in a trance-like state long after nightfall.

Despite the description of Lina that Lang provided to Ting, she could not spot her anywhere near the information booth of Shanghai Port. She searched for two hours throughout the port, afraid to leave in case Lina was just running late. The night began to fall, and still, Ting was alone. She trusted Lang, so there was no reason for him to lie to her about Lina's arrival. She wondered if there was another exit in the harbor but the port authorities assured her that she was at the only exit for arriving ships. Ting promptly realized that communication with the Shanghai people was problematic. Growing up in Huangyan meant Ting could not easily understand the Shanghai dialect. She once mocked their formal tone while sitting in the cafeteria with DanDan. Ting now realized it may have been helpful to study it. She had studied English since a young age and was just barely competent enough to employ it in a real-life situation. The skill was useless to her at this very moment in time. Ting walked out of the port, terrified. She was alone in this monstrously huge city, with no one to call and no place to go. She began to walk towards the lights that illuminated nearby skyscrapers and cast a shadow on the smaller, more traditional structures below. These old streets weaved around the modern towers like snakes and depicted the sharp contrast between new and old China. Citizens could not adapt to the rate of development and often gave up any hopes of trying. It was evident from the architecture and style of Shanghai that it was an exceptional and colossal titan. Ting soon reached Nanjing Road, a famous pedestrian street in the city. She gazed in pure happiness at the vast array of clothing and technology stores. The large electronic banners warmed her skin as her head swiveled to take in each one. Within a split second, Ting immediately froze. Her mouth dropped as she witnessed a group of white foreigners exiting one of the megastores. This was the first time that Ting had seen an outsider in person, let alone a group of them. She was stunned by their fair complexions. Their eyes seemed huge. They appeared as if they were going to fall right out of their heads. They spoke in a language that Ting could not understand and cackled like hyenas as they bounced throughout the walking street, arms covered to the shoulders with shopping bags filled with clothing. One of them looked at her and blew a kiss as he winked. She stood paralyzed in wonder.

Alone and lost in the center of Shanghai, Ting peered into her bag to examine the rolls of red bills Captain Lang had given her before she left. She exited the pedestrian street and began to search for a low-cost hotel to spend the night. After walking through dozens of dimly-lit side streets and marketplaces, she found a cozy little hotel tucked away in an alley between a supermarket and a small shopping mall. Dark, slender trees swayed slowly in front of the hotel. When Ting looked down the block, she saw a small group of vendors. Smoke emanated from their grills and rose to wrap around their faces. The hotel was not the extravagant and luxurious castle she had pictured while she was on the ship, but she now needed to survive by any means necessary. This was especially considering that Lina was nowhere to be found. Ting wondered again as to what kind of fate could have befallen her, but she didn't even know Lina and couldn't waste much more time thinking of her. The hotel had Wi-Fi and Ting would be able to recuperate for a few days and establish herself in Shanghai from there, as the hotel's fees were more than reasonable and she had plenty of money available for the time being. Ting checked in and proceeded upstairs to her room. Turning off the lamp on the desk, she stared lovingly out of the window over the vast expanse of concrete and the surplus of city lights. She curled up on her bed and closed her eyes, hopeful for the first time to see what the next day would bring.

CHAPTER SIX

Harry returned to his apartment community in the afternoon to find that the group of teachers had already gathered there. It was their second day off of the week. They surrounded a defenseless picnic table and quickly suffocated it with cold beer bottles.

"You guys are crazy. You're already drinking, this early in the day?"

"Yeah, it's sunny today," replied Shaniya.

"I wanted to know how much it would cost to cover this table in beer bottles. It cost six dollars," said Markin.

"And as you can see, Colleen is alive," stated Jonathan.

"If only Kevin were here with us right now. He used to spend his Tuesdays here with us," Shaniya remarked.

"Who's Kevin?" asked Harry.

"Hah! He's living in fairy land, don't even worry about him," replied Shaniya.

The truth was that Kevin Hallsby was a former teacher at the Happy Family English school. Educators and expats in China did not typically have stable lives in China and tended to filter out every couple of months. Expats that arrived in China as students would usually leave after one or two semesters, those that came for work would either finish their contracts or simply disappear in the middle of the night to return home in a panic, and even those that climbed the ranks in their professions did not seem to last long. It could, however, be said that at least half of the Happy Family English School staff were lifers, but the other half would most likely vanish within months. Upon Kevin's departure from the school, the group had begun to mention Kevin nostalgically, as if he had suddenly died. He was, in fact, alive and well.

Kevin was known as the "one percent" of foreigners in China. He moved away from the Shanghai suburbs to a non-polluted city in southern China and had been there, happily married to a Chinese woman, for over four years. That was four times the life expectancy of a typical American-Chinese marriage. His former colleagues discovered that he was living a genuinely happy life there, without the dramatic affairs that often went hand in hand with the mentally unstable expat population. He and his wife were raising two young boys in their spacious apartment, located just minutes from the ocean. They were working less than twenty hours a week and still easily managed to live comfortably. This lifestyle was out of reach for most expats in China and was out of sight and out of mind for most of the staff at the Happy Family English School. They seldom spoke of Kevin, as he reminded them of the elusive stability that was nearly unattainable to them.

"Yeah, he's living the life... but what about Lynn, remember him?" asked Jonathan, sharply reminding the group of the other side of the expat spectrum.

Harry shifted in his seat but refrained from prying into the conversation this time. He listened and collected information about Lynn from their discussion.

He learned that the local expat community often referred to Lynn Davis by his nickname, "Sypha-lyn." This was in reference to his struggle with a variety of sexually transmitted diseases, one of which included syphilis. He was a Vietnam veteran from England and had spent over 15 years in Shanghai with his wife, who was a native Chinese citizen. His face was droopy and red. Lynn's eyes were cold and unexpressive. His clothes were often soaked and sweaty. Small drops of sweat would flow in meandering paths, from his forehead to his chin before flinging themselves away from his despicable face. His fingers trembled, and he smelled of cabbage. Lynn's wife could hardly stand spending any time with the appalling man at all. They had married for love, but for his wife, love was not as powerful as wealth. She forced Lynn to purchase apartments for her, and then for her parents. He was then pressured into buying a four-bedroom suite for her disabled sister, and later on, a studio apartment for her dog.

Lynn crumbled under his wife's demands and quickly turned to alcohol and prostitutes to quiet his mind. He eventually developed gonorrhea and chlamydia, in addition to syphilis, and would not get so much as a handshake from anyone who knew him. Lynn's brain began to deteriorate at a rapid pace. The disease had not been detected by the local doctors in a timely manner, and most of Lynn's cognitive functions were soon lost. His last night in Shanghai was devastating to both the expat community as well as the bankers who serviced the mortgages for his many apartments. That evening, Lynn was spotted by locals, running towards the Yangpu bridge. The illness had degraded his brain to the point of mental retardation and Lynn, in a deranged fit of insanity, threw his own body right over the edge. The expat community mourned the death but soon emptied any memory of Lynn from their narcissistic minds. He reminded them of the inevitable demise and fragile mortality that they all shared with him.

Harry was still far from comprehending the intricacies of the lifestyle here. Feeling much better than a couple of hours earlier, Harry sat down next to Dean at the wooden table.

"I guess I'll have a beer," he exhaled, "you guys are crazy."

"You shouldn't joke about that," replied Jonathan.

Jonathan began spouting a lengthy spiel about the difficulties many Westerners would face when moving to China and mentioned that it was rather challenging for most to find qualified psychiatrists. This stemmed from the widely-accepted idea that China's developments in mental health had barely exceeded those in its atrocious public hygiene. He mentioned that if Lynn had received proper care, or at least psychiatric assistance, he may still be alive.

"Holy shit," murmured Dean as he tightened his eyes.

"Excuse me, Dean, but I've had quite enough of your constant mockeries against me. What have I ever done to you?" asked Jonathan, removing his glasses as he revealed the outlandishly stern look on his face.

"I will literally reach my arm down your throat and rip out your stomach and feed it back to you through your throat into the empty hole that will be where your stomach once was," he replied.

"So hostile…"

"Relax everyone, I've got shots!" screamed Markin, while dribbling saliva down his blue polo shirt.

Markin had been drunk since late afternoon the night before and hadn't slept since. He hesitantly admitted that his night after the KTV consisted of attempting, rather unsuccessfully, to have sex with a group of about eight women in the middle of a public road. He boasted that there was a warrant out for his arrest by the police. This would have been a concern to the Happy Family English

School, but warrants and other files were often misplaced and forgotten by the police. This was especially true of crimes that had not actually been committed yet. Harry forced down the shot of the seahorse drink that some locals called *haimagong*. He was told that the bottles were shipped from southern China, brewed during an extended fermentation period. During that time, dozens of seahorse corpses would be shredded and diluted into the liquid. He took a swig of beer to empty his mouth of the taste.

"What the fuck is that?!"

Harry was peering over Colleen's shoulder when he noticed an elderly woman holding an infant over a garbage can. The child was wearing one-piece pajamas, light blue in color, with a long-slit cut into the bottom seam of the pants. This exposed the child as he hovered over the receptacle in the hands of his crazed grandmother.

"That's a baby shitting into a trash can," said Colleen.

"Oh, yeah, it happens. The Chinese don't think it's strange because it's just a baby. I've even seen them lay down newspapers and have their kids squat over them," commented Jonathan.

Dean let out a long belch directly into YuPi's face before walking over to a large tree. He urinated and proceeded to spit onto the nearby sidewalk. YuPi sat unfazed, though few teachers could recall why he was even there with them in the first place and still, no one cared to even ask.

The group sat, unenthusiastically, wasting the day away drunk, while the world around them sped on. They were detached from the society they were living in, and their careless nature was scarcely understood by the natives that tried to communicate with them.

An elderly Chinese man caught a glimpse of the group while taking an afternoon stroll through the community. He wandered towards Harry, noticing that he was the only one within the group that was in the same age range as him. Upon asking Harry where he was from, the man soon realized that no one in this group was capable of speaking Mandarin, the national language of the country in which they were all residing. The man smiled kindly and began to retreat, ignoring Colleen's commendable attempts to make conversation and show respect to the man in his native language.

"So, what are you guys planning for today?" asked Harry.

"I've gotta see a urologist," mentioned Markin.

"Lenny is coming up from Fujian today," said Shaniya, excitedly.

"What? I thought he went back to the states already," replied Colleen.

"No, he moved down there for another job, remember? He has a business meeting here in Shanghai this week, I told you guys about it a couple of weeks ago."

"I thought he was dead," murmured Dean.

"Is that someone who used to work here?" asked Harry.

"Yeah, he left around the same time that Kevin did. We need to take him out tonight. Let's go to the *hutong*," said Jonathan.

"Yes. Absolutely."

Hutong was a name given to the ancient streets of Chinese cities, those that still maintained the architecture of the past. In modern day China, *hutongs* had become cultural relics, and tourists would often flood these streets at all hours of the day. Touring these corridors was a chance to catch a glimpse of traditional life. Many people still lived in the houses and shops that lined these narrow walkways. Harry soon went up to his apartment for a short nap, while his co-workers continued to devour every single bottle on the picnic table. They seemed to excel in embracing the habits that Harry had spent the last several months trying to change. This was disheartening to Harry and reminded him of how weak he had become, unable to resist the devil's elixir. This internal conflict of his was also brewing so soon after his heated divorce, which was arguably caused by his uncontrollable drinking habits in the first place. The idea that Shanghai was not the place to mend his broken heart was growing stronger in his mind, but he was here and refused to spend every minute dwelling on the past. The past did, however, still creep in from time to time. Alcohol was as prevalent as herpes among the foreigners here, and every drop of liquor consumed seemed to seep between the cracks in Harry's broken heart.

As soon as Harry closed his eyes to nap, a sharp knocking sound startled him, and he carefully rose to his feet to investigate the source. Harry approached the living room door and realized that the knocking was not knocking at all, but a hammering. He didn't know what to do or what to expect. Harry grabbed the nearest object he could find and stood in front of the door, grasping an old, dusty lamp. He waited, panting nervously. Within a couple of minutes, the hammering at the door stopped. Harry walked over and looked through the peephole, though he spotted nothing but an empty hallway. He stepped back and turned the doorknob to peer into the corridor, but he was unable to open the door. He jiggled the doorknob, he rattled the top lock, and he then violently shook both simultaneously. He was locked in.

The electronic rent deposit for Harry's apartment had been paid by the school the week before his arrival but had not yet been transferred to the landlord's account. Unaware of the payment having been made, the landlord had trampled up the stairs to Harry's apartment and bolted his door firmly shut. This would prevent this white devil from enjoying the comforts of the apartment without having paid the rent, but unbeknown to the landlord, Harry was now trapped inside. He threw his shoulder into the door, hoping to knock it open but it was no use. He looked out of the window to see if there was a fire escape readily available. The apartment building was decades old, and at the time of construction, fire escapes were not thought of as necessary components in a habitable structure. Were there to be an actual fire in his apartment at this very moment, Harry would be facing certain death. He pulled himself back toward the wall of the living room and charged at the door to no avail. Harry tried once more, and the door frame shook loose. On the third attempt, he managed to knock the door clean off the hinges and soon after collapsed atop the wooden panel. Laying there, tired and nearly motionless, Harry listened as footsteps rose up the stairs and approached him.

"Hey man, you wanna come down? I'm about to go down to the table, some of the guys are out there drinking," said Ricardo.

"I was already down there. I was just trying to nap, but it seems that's not going to happen."

"Sleep when you're dead, man. That's what I always say."

"Ok, fine, let's go," replied Harry.

As Ricardo and Harry descended the building's stairway and stepped outside, they could see Dean screaming quite violently at a small hoard of security guards. The apartment community's security staff had been notified that a large group of foreigners was loitering around the picnic table reserved for Dr. Wang and his friends. Dr. Wang was an old, retired professor that had spent 59 years teaching at the Shanghai College of Japanese Studies. The college offered several classes in Sino-Japanese history ranging from *Japanese Provocation in War 121* to *Faults of Japanese Culture 222*. The classes went all the way up to the advanced level, and Dr. Wang had created the highest-level class offered, *Chinese Superiority in Morality and Technology 450*. China's hatred for Japan had stemmed from centuries of ongoing conflicts and wars with the country, and since the end of World War II, a stagnant type of resentment remained, lingering within the Chinese population. The hatred was exacerbated by the fact that the government and CCTV channels often portrayed Japan in a negative light. China had authorized the creation of nearly a century's worth of films that depicted China's significant victories over the monstrous invaders. Nearing 90 years old, Dr. Wang was a stubborn old man, but he often rejoiced during the time he spent with his old friends. They often played poker outside and maintained an unofficial reservation of the picnic table nearly every sunny afternoon.

The security guards approached the group of teachers in the hopes of freeing this table for Dr. Wang, kindly ignoring the fact that it was trashed and littered with emptied beer bottles. Dean had begun to argue with the guards, though his Chinese level was low and his shouting was falling on deaf ears. The guards stood, shocked, that their straightforward and minor request for a favor was being received so harshly. Colleen quickly stepped in and settled the dispute, notifying the group that they needed to clear the table and head out. Dean thought the whole situation was outrageous, as an outdoor picnic table in an apartment community shouldn't be reserved for any reason, but Colleen understood the power of relationships in China. She understood *guanxi*. Colleen, Shaniya, and Jonathan cleared off the table as Ricardo, Harry, Dean, and Markin planned for the night ahead. Lenny was going to be in Shanghai at any minute, and that was as good of a reason as any to plan a big night out. As conversations concluded, Ricardo left the area. He retreated to his apartment for his ritual-like grooming that usually preceded a night out. The other teachers soon followed suit. Markin looked back at Harry as he left. His left eye glimmered, his right eye wandered.

CHAPTER SEVEN

Ting found herself awake earlier than usual. Her fascination with Shanghai generated an excitement that couldn't keep her asleep until dawn. She rose with a great hunger that needed to be satisfied. Ting planned to buy new clothes and create a resume to secure a job as quickly as possible. She exited the hotel lobby and quickly glanced back at the vacant front desk. When she stepped outside, a crazed beggar was draped over a wet stack of cardboard boxes. The horrifying stench of liquor and urine brushed against Ting's tongue. The darkness of the night still veiled the dull buildings and potential dangers lurked behind every corner. Shanghai was dangerous but it was vast and every building, every interaction, and every day held great opportunity. Ting was eager for success, but first, she needed to grab a quick bite to eat. She marched outside, walking briskly. Ting needed to find proper sustenance if she was to work hard preparing for her future. After several blocks, she found a small three story building that was lit up by pink neon signs. Several men were eating outside of the dark restaurant, and Ting decided to get a quick bite to eat there. She stepped inside, first through the steel door and then through the wooden one. She entered what appeared to be an empty building, and the restaurant's tables were out of sight. Ting found several menu books laying on the counter. This was a rather odd restaurant to her. In Huangyan, not an inch of a restaurant would be spared. Owners usually put every available space to use. A young man immediately rushed over to Ting and shouted for her to go upstairs. He held a notebook in his hand that Ting confused for a waiter's pad and she abided, though she still couldn't understand his strange Shanghai dialect.

Ting heard a quiet bustling upstairs and was excited to see what kind of restaurant she had found. It was probably a popular location since it was filled with people so early in the day. The young man brought her up the fading carpeted stairs and held a large sign to her face. The sign was about the size of a sheet of paper, white in color, and read "7" in bold text. She held the sign in her hands, waiting for her number to be called so that she could place her order. This seemingly organized system impressed Ting, who had never had to queue in line before.

In Huangyan, every government office, restaurant, and store contained massive, dead-eyed flocks of people, staring at their phones and gently pushing and scuffling for their turn. Ting's favorite restaurant back home was named "Silver Spike Lucky Eats," and although it was often crowded, all varieties of food could be found there. Most of the treats were grilled on thin, metal skewers. She sometimes visited the restaurant with DanDan, who would spend nearly an hour talking with the owner, hoping to receive a small discount. They would scan the black, metallic grills, inspecting the quality of various meats. Grilled squid, fish, pork, beef, crab, chicken, meatballs, oysters, shrimp, scorpions, spiders, millipedes, dog, cockroaches, and lamb penis filled both the indoor and outdoor seating area with a broad spectrum of scents. Chefs carefully selected live baby mice and directed waiters to deliver bowls of them to guests. The critters were meticulously prepared and served with a distinct dipping sauce. Thick red oils filled deep, white community bowls and contained hidden treasures beneath the pepper-flaked surface. The restaurant reminded them of the *hutong* that they grew up in. Familiar sights and scents always brought back those memories.

The restaurant appeared to be always busy, with every table full every night of the week. Those that could not be seated simply ordered skewers and stood in front of the outdoor seating area, casually snacking. Many of the patrons ate and drank until their stomachs bulged like a baboon's ass. Occasionally, guests would get caught up in confrontations with members of their own party, battling for the right to pay the bill. Traditional customs dictated that the wealthiest member of the dinner party would treat his lesser guests to dinner by paying the total amount. Guests would playfully fight for the chance and opportunity to hold this honor, though playful arguments often turned to wrestling matches between men. At least one table was broken each night, as drunk husbands fought for the bill and inevitably lost their footing. The outdoor area was exciting but often trashed. It was customary to throw scraps and garbage onto the table as well as the ground. This would make the cleaning process easier for the waitresses that could sweep the entire restaurant grid with a couple of wide brooms. Ting and DanDan would sit there for hours to people-watch and fill up on meats. These were rare occasions for them, considering their low salaries and limited free time.

Ting snapped out of the past and looked back down at the young man. He grabbed the number out of Ting's hand and hung it by a string around her neck so that the number could be correctly displayed on her chest. She was confused as to why he had done this, but since she was a stranger in this highly-developed and modern city, she understood that she needed to learn their customs. The man opened a side channel of the hallway and pushed Ting through the door. She soon realized she was in a line-up with nine other girls. The girls were dressed rather promiscuously, and some wore skirts that revealed their lower buttocks. Some were hardly covered at all. Their faces looked like chalk-covered sidewalks in a rainstorm. White powder and black mascara dripped from the eyes of number 3. Number 2 wore torn stockings and a black, leather miniskirt. Her hair was messy, and she had a glazed-over, cold look on her face. Number 9 was crying. Number 1 was undoubtedly drugged. She danced slowly and pulled at her top while staring at the ceiling. A few of the women wore transparent clothing. Some wore thin spaghetti straps, but at the sound of a buzzer, they all began to remove their tops.

"Do any of you know where I can place my order? What kind of restaurant is this?" asked Ting.

"Shut up you damn idiot, you're going to spoil my earnings for the night," replied 8.

"Quiet you ugly, village wench," shouted 6.

"All of you shut up, you're going to dry me out like a fried dumpling," yelled 2.

"Dry like a fried dumpling? Yeah, maybe the way your old, whore mother makes them, you bitch," replied 6.

Ting had mistakenly slipped into one of Shanghai's darkest underworlds. She had walked into a brothel rather than a restaurant, and the realization hit her like a moving train. Ting often heard of the brothels in Huangyan but had never seen one in person. She was aware that her co-workers at the factory worked in one, but they never spoke of it, as

104

openly admitting to acts of prostitution was considered dishonorable. In comparison to the brothels in Huangyan, this building was huge and filled with guests in even the latest hours of the night. The women in the line-up were prostitutes that slept all day and earned quite a living during the evening. Ting became worried that the police would raid the room at any moment and mistake her for a worker, unaware that several police officers were already on the other side of the mirrored glass, debating on which women to hire for the night. She turned and pushed the door. It didn't open. She began to walk toward the other side of the narrow room, squeezing herself between the glass and the women. Some of the prostitutes pushed her away, and their decrepit breasts roughly grazed Ting's face. Ting was rudely pushed past number 2 and turned back to look at the face of the girl labeled "3". The girl had incredibly bright and beautiful eyes and wore an embroidered, red skirt. She wiped the running mascara from her eyes with her left hand that had a large birthmark on it. She looked at Ting with a stone-cold stare and took off her black framed glasses. Ting recalled the description of the large and unique birthmark.

"What the fuck are you looking at?"

"...Lina?"

"How do you know my-"

Another girl threw Ting towards the door. The sharp movement tore the whore's short skirt and momentarily revealed her mangled genitals. A man from the other side of the glass began to shout on the loudspeaker. Ting started towards the far exit of the room, accelerating frantically. The doorknob was unlocked, but it was stuck. She fumbled and desperately panicked to open it, knocking her hip against it until it eventually came loose. She was finally able to escape. Shouting still echoed in the distance as Ting scrambled through a maze of dark hallways, trying to find an exit while avoiding populated areas of the brothel. She threw her number on the floor and proceeded down the stairs at a rapid pace, sobbing. Exiting the building, Ting realized there was much to learn in Shanghai. She needed to study the Shanghainese dialect as well as standard Mandarin pronunciation to communicate effectively with others. She needed to become accustomed to her surroundings and understand that this massive city was certainly not like home.

Lina's situation was still unclear to Ting. She wondered whether Lina had been kidnapped and forced into prostitution or whether she had abandoned her at Shanghai Port intentionally. The truth was that Lina had never even heard of Ting's plans to arrive in Shanghai. Being an old and traditionally-minded man, Captain Lang had notified her of Ting's arrival by sending a letter through the Chinese post, which had a delivery success rate of less than 50 percent. Lina had never received the letter and was therefore completely unaware that Ting even existed and that she was expected to meet her at the port.

Ting was frazzled, but determined, to continue with her plans. She ate breakfast and returned to the hotel, spending hours polishing her resume in the business room. Several other girls were using computers to photoshop photos of themselves to enlarge their eyes and whiten their skin. Ting continued working, and she also worked on perfecting her pronunciation of standard Mandarin. She printed the resume after highlighting years of experience at a successful and well-known corporate factory. Her high school "computer knowledge" class had been useful for something. As she folded the paper into her bag, she exited the hotel once more, pausing to acquire directions from one of the front desk staff members.

"Hello, do you know the fastest way to get to the walking street from here? I've only walked from there during the night," said Ting.

"Yes, take a right out of the hotel and then take a left and then a right at the restaurant."

"Which restaurant do I take the right turn at?"

"The noodle shop."

"Ok... and after that?"

"Then you can walk straight until you arrive."

These directions were, of course, complete nonsense but the staff member was new on the job and new in the area. Admitting a lack of knowledge was embarrassing but giving the wrong directions could hardly disrupt interpersonal harmony in the current moment. Ting understood this and headed back towards the city lights. She strolled from store to store in Shanghai's walking street for over an hour, carefully selecting the most fashionable, yet reasonably priced, work attire. She entered a shopping mall and glanced at the directory of stores in awe. Ting walked past the escalator as it soundlessly malfunctioned and quickly devoured the young couple that was standing on it. She heard their shrieks of horror and watched as they instantly fell to their deaths. They easily disappeared into the dark void. This often happened in China as buildings, escalators, and other mechanical inventions were built for pennies in a day and often lasted just as long. Ting finished shopping and stepped outside, trotting carelessly through the courtyards. She was seated at an outdoor cafe a couple of blocks from the busy street and was finally able to relax with clothing and resume in hand. She looked at the pedestrians and began to feel like a city person- arms exhausted from being weighed down by shopping bags. People in Shanghai seemed to move so fast. Every minute there was a dollar to be made and every wasted hour brought a person one step closer to homelessness. Ting observed everything. She spotted wailing children scattered throughout the street, riding atop their parents' shoulders. Beggars sat, staring at moving cars, rattling their tin cups against the wind. Shanghai's tourist elite pranced through the streets as the city folk worked. They peered through shop windows and shouted at how cheap everything was. Ting looked towards her hotel, which was located much farther away from the shops and glamor. The garbage cans that lined the streets were overflowing, the sky was hazy, and the streets were loud and congested, but Ting was happy. She looked toward the fading stars as the Shanghai sun situated itself high in between the clouds.

CHAPTER EIGHT

Harry snapped back into consciousness. The lights beaming down from the top of the room blinded him. He looked down. He was holding two playing cards. The back of the cards read "Golden Dragon Club." The high, Shanghai sun crept through one of the tiny windows that lined the ceiling. The club was about to close soon, and some patrons began to file out of the building. The stocky man sitting across the table from Harry was shrouded in a cloud of cigarette smoke. His head was as broad and rigid as a shipping container, and his gold teeth reflected the ceiling lights as he cackled. Saliva fired out of his mouth onto the table. The stocky man pushed all his chips into the center of the table and laughed once more. The man to the right of him looked like a shriveled, old condom. He was so weak and elderly that he was hardly able to sit upright. The feeble man used his chair to shovel his animated corpse closer to the green felt and pushed his chips into the center of the table. He turned to face the next man, who sat in a contemplative pose. His sunglasses were reflective and nearly translucent. He held a single chicken wing in his left hand. He ate while he played and spoke while he ate. With his right hand, he pushed his chips into the center of the table. Two other players threw their cards to the dealer, one of which said he was leaving to see if the pink, neon brothel down the street was still open. The dealer sat smiling, and the remaining players looked towards Harry.

Harry lifted his drink to his mouth and poured half of it onto his tongue while the other half fell into his lap. He stood up in a panic, and his eyes widened as alcohol dripped from his pants. He rose so quickly that his thighs caught on the table and leaned it toward the stocky man, tilting a table full of chips, drinks, cards, and cell phones. The man was covered, and Harry's mouth dropped. The wide oak stood carefully, wiping brown liquor from his shirt. The shriveled, old condom winced. The man with the sunglasses and chicken wing walked away. Harry turned and started to slowly creep away as he felt a firm hand on his shoulder. The sturdy giant squeezed Harry's shoulder as he collapsed onto the ground. Within moments, there was a group of about six crazed gamblers beating Harry to a pulp. When he awoke once more, he was lying in a pile of black garbage bags that were tucked away in an alley, with the hot afternoon sun pelting his leathered skin.

The previous night, Markin and the group had gathered to take Lenny out, since he was in town on business for only a short time. They arrived at a brewery near the center of Shanghai just after dinner. It was then that they had come across Daniel Hodges and his wife. They were sipping club soda to wet their thin, pale lips and their eyes radiated excitement as they saw the group approaching.

Daniel was an anomaly within the expat subculture of Shanghai. He had been in the city for nearly eight years, living with his wife, Noreen, and his three children, Zebedee, Ezekiel, and Faith. The Hodges lived a surprisingly Western lifestyle in Shanghai. They purchased a three-bedroom apartment in the quiet, modern district of the city. They opened a small business in the adjacent apartment that was divided into both a bakery and a yoga studio. The couple had even hosted several holiday dinners for Thanksgiving and Christmas. Most interestingly of all, Daniel and Noreen had organized Sunday prayer and Bible discussion meetings that would convene every week inside the bakery, behind closed doors. These meetings were open, by invitation only, to both Westerners and Chinese citizens and were discretely aimed at spreading the word of Christianity to the godforsaken country. Being from Georgia, they were outspoken simpletons, easily fooled by words written by deluded desert scribes just 2000 years earlier. They were aware that Chinese officials had unofficially outlawed "God" decades ago and lived their lives with the sole purpose of bringing hope back to the hopeless. In a way, the family considered themselves missionaries without a sect, but many also labeled them religious vigilantes. Daniel and Noreen's closest friend was Dr. Steve Rogers, who was hired to work at the International Clinic of the municipal hospital in Shanghai. Most of his acquaintances and patients had grown accustomed to simply referring to him as Dr. Steve. The doctor was tasked with training the Chinese medical staff, who had long been accustomed to prescribing false medicines and other forms of witchcraft to their patients at exuberant prices. This was a new custom for Dr. Steve, who previously thrived on charging thousands of dollars for simple check-ups in America, rather than by prescribing magical serums. For the Chinese staff, these potions were the cure for ailments as well as for their unsubstantial paychecks. For broken legs, they advised patients to dab alcohol onto the affected area. For other maladies and infections, they suggested that patients drink more hot water to cure their pains. Psychological issues in patients were often, in their minds, resolved by a modest suggestion to "relax more often." Patients that required minor surgeries would have to provide the surgeon with a one-time gift in the form of a padded, red envelope. Doing so would ensure that the doctor paid the utmost attention during the procedure. For severe traumas that required immediate and critical care, doctors would often go on break to avoid the situation altogether. Dr. Steve's mission in China was to modernize the International Clinic of the hospital, though he was also a main accomplice to the underground activities and meetings frequently organized by the Hodges family. The Hodges' children were brainwashed at a young age, taught to obey the word of their "God," as it was interpreted by their parents. They were home schooled, though they adopted the customs of the Chinese incredibly quickly at their young age. They were, however, prohibited from bringing any Chinese members of the opposite sex to the apartment. Although Daniel and Noreen thought they were saving these people from eternal damnation, they admitted that the Chinese would never be completely absolved of their sins considering they "were born godless and would likely die godless."

Aside from these ideas, shrouded in lunacy, Daniel and his wife projected an aura of the standard American suburban family. When customers entered their bakery, they were greeted with coffee and a menu, not to mention the ear-piercing small talk that often manifested itself within suburban housewives. Daniel's very essence repulsed Markin, Shaniya, Ricardo, Dean, and nearly every other Westerner that came across him. For the group, who thrived on the vices and spoils of China, working only several hours a week for thrice the pay of their Chinese counterparts, a symbol of morality was the last thing they wished to encounter. Ricardo had long seen the Hodges as a cult-like group of imbeciles, hell bent on spewing their verbal poisons onto anyone that would listen. He couldn't get even a single word into a conversation with Daniel or Noreen without it somehow leading to Jesus dying on the cross again. Noreen, on the other hand, was repulsed by the pure vulgarity of the godless Americans that were in her midst. To her, it seemed every second was spent cursing or talking about the disgusting act of sexual intercourse. She was a born-again virgin ever since her third child and second abortion and she made sure everyone knew about the excellent opportunities available to create second chances in life.

She looked at the group of miscreants and waved in false excitement. Ricardo and Dean's eyes sank while Markin immediately walked off toward the bar.

"Gosh it is great to see y'all!" shrieked Noreen, as her fluorescent-white, rodent-like teeth crept over her bottom lip.

"Hey guys, have a great night, we're just going to go sit by the bar," replied Ricardo, ending the conversation as quickly as it began and sparing the entire group from her empty formalities.

From there, the night progressed as usual, with half of the teachers drinking to near paralysis and the other half managing to

117

somehow injure themselves on the way home. Ricardo and Harry wandered back toward their apartment complex at around four in the morning. They stopped at the nearby outdoor barbecue on the way. Ricardo attempted to communicate with the owner of the eatery in the hopes of ordering some late-night snacks, but while leaning on the wooden display table, collapsed. The arrangement consisted of a mosaic of raw meats and seafood waiting to be grilled. By placing his hand on the buffet to lean against it, Ricardo's hand slipped, causing him to crash through the wooden plank. The table flipped over and landed on top of him, covering him in the meats and drenching him in the raw juices. As he lay on the ground, soaked, he endured endless berating from the outraged owners. They harshly scolded him for ruining their nightly earnings. Harry stood with a glazed-over look on his face, sipping from his beer bottle and waiting for the situation to be over. Ricardo was forced to pay 30 dollars to cover the costs of the food wasted. He retreated home shortly after. The owners then washed the meats and ordered them to be placed on a sturdier table. Harry walked back towards the main road and hailed a cab instead of going upstairs and retiring for the night. He wanted to go back to the brewery and see if his flask was still there, realizing he had forgotten it only after returning to the apartment community with Ricardo.

That was about all that Harry could remember as he rolled over to prop his body upwards. The events that followed must have somehow led him to the underground casino. Lying in piles of garbage was more comfortable than it seemed, though, he thought. He stood up, dazed, and left the alley while the hot Shanghai sun baked the remaining brain cells in his head. He stood on the busy street and checked his phone, it was dead. Life in the city continued, despite Harry standing motionless in the middle of the sidewalk. In the distance, he spotted a vendor and began to approach him hoping that he would be able to quench his thirst and force the throbbing in his head to subside. The vendor was slender, with dark, sun-scarred skin and bushy gray eyebrows. His shorts were torn, and his shirt was tied around his head to protect him from the rays of the sun. Harry looked at the vendor's face in confusion as his mouth began to ooze a thick, bright red liquid. He spat, projecting the vile, red mucus that pelted his right thigh. The vendor was chewing *binglang*, often referred to around Southeast Asia as "betel nut." The betel nut, as it was internationally called, was really the seed of the areca palm tree and was known for its psycho-hallucinogenic effects on the human body. The intense nicotine-like high that it produced had been thrashing the vendor's mouth and throat with carcinogens for decades and the damaging effects were instantly visible to Harry. Regardless, Harry was intrigued. He motioned to the man to give him two pieces. The man's eyes slowly widened, realizing for the first time that he was looking directly into the eyes of a white man. The vendor's mouth widened into a smile as more of the thick liquid dripped from his teeth. Harry motioned for two pieces once again, and the man began to cut and roll the betel nut inside of dark-green leaves.

Harry walked the streets in a state of nervousness and confusion, obviously affected to an incredible extent by the extreme power of the *binglang*. He felt his heart racing and sat on a park bench to recuperate. He drank from the water fountain and relaxed for several minutes, allowing his heart to slow and his mind to calm. The park was beautiful during midday and accommodated locals of all ages. The elderly often gambled or practiced *taiji* while their grandchildren sat together nearby, eating insects and vomiting shortly after. Couples strolled throughout the paved pathways of the park and held hands. Musicians gathered and plucked their instruments until they resonated the sounds of an old culture, sacred and unscathed. Before long, he dozed off and had begun to dream. His wife was cooking an English breakfast in the kitchen, and the warm smell of the baked beans lightly caressed his fluffy beard. The sunlight entered the living room through the skylight and birds soothingly sang the songs of spring. Harry was younger and alert, with his whole life ahead of him. His entire adventure had merely begun, and he would spend it with his best friend and soul mate. He entered the kitchen and removed several eggs from the carton, handing them to his wife.

"You may need these if you're going to cook an English breakfast," he said with a modest smile on his face.

"Oh, is that right?"

"Yep, you know, I'm one of the best cooks in the state. Do you remember who won the Mad-Wing Cook-off Festival last summer?"

"Right, right, right. Well, I definitely know who will be talking about it for the next thirty years," she remarked.

"Yeah, yeah. So, are we going to take care of the car today?" he asked.

"We should, but I wanted to ask you when you wanted to book those tickets for Bali, did you order your new surfboard yet or will you rent one there?"

"I need to check when our winter vacation dates are. My students need a lot of help before I can think about vacation. Sometimes I think I can really get through to some of them if only they would apply themselves," Harry said.

"You are so sweet. Now I remember why I married you."

"I thought it was because of my stellar performance in the sack."

"If I were looking for that, I would have married one of your brothers... Actually-"

"Which one, Danny with the double chin or Robby with the third ball? They still piss themselves, you know?" he interrupted, jokingly.

"Yeah, I know. Do you have the babble?"

"What?"

"The babble from the place we went to yesterday."

"I..."

"The booble dabs, did you get them?"

"Honey? What?"

"The scadoobie thing with ladles and sugar plum."

"What do you mean?"

"The bappy dings with the wing flings and a hot floor bopper. You know the bam bam bam bam bam bam bam."

Harry sprung out of the dream as his head dropped backward on the park bench. He heard familiar voices approaching and turned his head towards the noise, spotting Markin's shiny bald head from a distance. The other teachers were also there, laughing at him. They had decided to take a walk through the park before beginning the next night of festivities, despite having to work the following day.

"Man, if you begin to look any more depressed, you're going to end up like Lance," Markin mentioned.

Markin was, of course, referring to a teacher from the "White Baby English Center." Lance was a walking representation of the Napoleon complex. He had been suffering from a particular type of "masculine

123

jealousy" for years in America. Before long, Lance finally decided to move to Shanghai and level the playing field. His situation led him to develop a general agitation with most people, and he often became violent with other male teachers to compensate for his minuscule manhood. He began searching for a Chinese girlfriend instantly in the hopes of finally impressing a woman with his limited arsenal. The girl that Lance finally did find had never been with a foreign man before. She made Lance the happiest person on earth by sleeping with him on the third date instead of fleeing in a fit of laughter. Chinese men often sat in wonder at the taste of such Americans, who would select Chinese woman based on seemingly no logical pattern at all. The women who were considered beautiful to the Chinese were mediocre to the Americans and the women the Chinese considered "leftovers" were often found desirable to foreign men. Lance's girlfriend could have easily been considered the latter. She was hardly considered beautiful or intelligent by either group and lacked proper etiquette in nearly all public situations. When Lance would bring her to dinner with his co-workers, she spat fish bones from her mouth directly onto the table. She would often raise her leg onto the dining table and belch into the air, smiling while revealing her crooked front tooth. When Lance took her to the movies, the troll talked the entire time and funneled popcorn into her pimpled, fat face. She would then ask Lance to take her home and would pretend to be exhausted and uninterested for ten minutes, before finally bedding him. The wicked woman moaned like a ghost as she experienced Lance's gherkin and he couldn't have been any happier. He was in love, but soon, his love life had come to an end. The girlfriend met an incredibly tragic fate, being trampled to death by a herd of cars during rush hour while crossing the street. She hadn't looked upwards even once as she stepped into the busy road and was killed almost immediately. Lance stood on the sidewalk in a rather relaxed state of shock, quoting his friend Nathan who used to say that "even if she's a one in a million kind of girl, there are still a thousand of them in China."

Harry looked back at the group.

"I'm not depressed, I'm just hungover. I'm not really supposed to be drinking like this anymore. This is one of the reasons my wife divorced me, hah," replied Harry.

"Dude, just find some tiny, little Chinese girl to hook up with," said Dean.

"I don't need that. I don't think I could handle another relationship right now."

"Aw, Harry. You'll be alright," said Shaniya.

"Man, are you crying?" asked Ricardo.

"No, I'm all right," replied Harry as he wiped a developing tear from the corner of his eye.

The group noticed that Harry was becoming emotional and human emotions were the last thing that they wanted to encounter. They were sociopaths and narcissists. Westerners that packed up their bags and moved across the world to China often did so with particularly selfish motives. Emotionally scarred and damaged from failed relationships back home, they left to stroke their egos abroad and try to finally come out on top. Many expats throughout China had left their homes in the United States, England, Australia, Canada, South Africa, and other mainly English-speaking countries to reap the rewards of China's booming economy. They wanted to be the biggest fishes in the pond. They also understood that the Western population in China was detached and often unable to form real friendships since many would not be residing in the country for long. The group of teachers changed the subject quickly and suggested that they all go to a nearby pub. The sun would set shortly, and most of the teachers soon decided to call out of work sick the next morning to extend their drunken weekend.

"Let's go to the Kona Bar," blurted Markin.

"Yeah! I'm up for some cheap beers. What band is playing tonight?" asked Ricardo.

"White Sugar," replied Colleen.

Markin couldn't go anywhere without stopping at a small shop to pick up a flask or two of their finest penis drinks. The group purchased several containers, ate a quick dinner of beef soup noodles, and returned to the shop once more to replenish their supply. They walked out of the store, carelessly throwing emptied bottles that shattered in the street. Harry looked up towards the moon, thinking of his wife. He then finished his flask before shattering it.

CHAPTER NINE

Ting finished her resume and rapidly arranged a job interview that was then scheduled for later in the day. After the interview, she came across a young girl about her own age. She got to talking with the girl, and they quickly became friends, finding that they had much in common. Hua came to Shanghai from a small city located only two hours from Huangyan, and the two spoke in the same dialect. Ting excitedly told Hua about her recent job interview. Hua evaluated and judged Ting's efforts as she had previously grown accustomed to doing with her other friends. Hua also passively remarked that the job was probably "good enough for now" and that Ting could find something better later, though Hua herself had never worked a day in her life. Ting reluctantly

129

continued and mentioned that she had seen the ad on a job board while browsing the computer in the hotel's business room. The Double Happy Good Smoke headquarters was hiring assistant manager trainees in Shanghai. The finding was a stroke of pure luck for Ting. She had already accumulated multiple years of experience working at the Double Happy Good Smoke factory of Huangyan and the headquarters in Shanghai was now offering a management-level position. She walked into an office that was located on the large main floor of a magnificent skyscraper. The administrative assistant took her resume and application for employment. The admin's eyes widened significantly as she looked over Ting's resume. Her mouth slowly dropped as she looked up.

"You worked in the Huangyan branch?"

"Yes, I did. I believe that my experiences there would make me a great fit for a position here at the headquarters. I am also loyal and hard-working."

"There was a small accident at the Huangyan factory today. You haven't heard?"

"No, I haven't. What do you mean?"

"The facility exploded this morning. It vaporized six city blocks."

"What are you talking about? Are you serious? What happened?" Ting frantically asked.

"I don't really know. I heard the engineers were replacing some sort of pressure tanks within the machinery when someone lit a cigarette, incinerating the entire area."

Ting gasped, retreating backward.

"Anyway, good luck on your interview today."

At the time, Ting was awestruck, and vivid memories of Huangyan immediately came rushing back to her. It was likely that everyone she had every known or worked with was now dead. Ting held the tears in. She went to the restroom to compose herself, hiding her emotions better than she had previously been able to do. Within minutes, she walked back outside into the waiting room with an aura of intensity and waited for the manager to be free of his duties. She had already left Huangyan in the rear-view mirror and would not let it come crawling forward now.

Hua grunted in affirmation, chewing on a grilled fish stick, as Ting continued to describe her experience. She mentioned that when she finally met the manager, he was kind, level-headed, and soon realized that Ting's expertise was certainly a useful addition to his managerial team. He had also previously visited the Huangyan branch of the company and was impressed by their high level of productivity. He still held their work ethic in high regard despite the terrible incident that had occurred just hours earlier. He hired her almost instantly, which surprised Ting, but this was a rather common practice in Shanghai. Employees had a high turnaround rate and were always looking for better opportunities in the big city. She was so overjoyed that she ran out of the headquarters' door jumping with excitement. It was almost as though everyone she had ever known back home was still alive and well. She rejoiced at her accomplishments. Within a day, she had found a temporary residence, explored a megacity, and had already been offered a job. She was stunned by the speed at which everything moved in Shanghai. Hua listened to her story apathetically as she pulled out her cell phone to reply to a few messages. She then walked away to answer a call. Ting's mood sank again. She began to think they didn't have as much in common as she had originally thought.

When Hua came back from her phone call, she told Ting that she wanted to take her to a pub just a couple of subway stops away. Ting had never been to a pub, but she was a strong, independent woman now, capable of anything. She wanted to try new things and meet new people, if only to network for her future. They boarded the subway at the nearest stop, and Ting stood in awe of the immense power of the metal serpents. The subways were so new and modern. They were air conditioned, clean, and lined wall to wall with flat screen televisions. They made the subways of even great cities like New York seem like trash cans on conveyor belts. The conductors came over the loud speakers to announce the next station, and after her short acclimation period, Ting could now understand the Shanghai dialect. After three stops on the subway, Hua pointed to the sliding doors, notifying Ting that they had arrived. They climbed the stairs to exit the station. After walking up and through the doors, Ting noticed that this part of Shanghai was completely different than the busy, downtown area she had been spending most of her time in. Despite them only having traveled three stops on the train, the city's atmosphere had changed drastically. Smoky fumes filled the air. The neighborhood was configured of old-style buildings that were plastered in brand new electronic screens and signs. Ting noticed that even though the skyline now hid in the distance, this part of the city was lively in its own way. Acrobats and dancers performed on a small stage at the end of the street. Vendors were set up in every crevice of the neighborhood. Much of the city's tattooed, rebellious youth also congregated on every street corner. Smoking and drinking, they crowded together blasting music from their phones. Punk music blared from several dark dens, and Ting listened to the sounds of clinking glasses escaping from within. Hua walked at a quickened pace and seemed to know the area very well, weaving through vendor carts and maneuvering the alleyways between bars. The smell of dried fish and other horrendous treasures from the sea was robust enough to sicken even the toughest Westerner, but these were familiar aromas to the locals. Ting followed Hua like a lost, abandoned dog. After about ten minutes of rapid scuffling and heavy panting, Hua told her that they had arrived. She read the dirty bar sign that appeared to be at the entrance of "Kona Bar." The bar was comfortable and dark, with warm purple light emanating from the ceiling. An enthusiastic band played hard rock on a small platform, and the patrons sang along at times. They shouted and often spilled beer and liquor onto the dark, hardwood floor.

When Ting walked into the smoke-filled room, she immediately noticed a large flock of foreigners sitting around an old wooden table towards the back of the bar. These pale invaders were everywhere, she thought. They were throwing their money around and drinking without a worry in the world. Long ago, she had heard of Chinese women dating and even marrying these foreigners, though the act was strictly forbidden by most traditional parents. She sat at the bar, far from the other customers and Hua went back outside to take a call. She noticed that one of the foreigners had a bald head like a billiards ball. His head was illuminated by the pub's florid ceiling lights. He seemed to be staring at a table of young girls and, in turn, whispering to a friend of his. The friend had a long ponytail and was grossly unshaven. His cargo shorts were dirty, and he was clearly intoxicated. The man reached for a flask out of one of his baggy pockets every few minutes. Another of them was an overweight black woman that was texting at the table with a huge grin glued to her face. She was obese and unattractive but had a handsome, young Chinese man sitting quietly beside her. It seemed several others were drinking and competing. Ting couldn't understand why these white devils felt the need to throw balls into glasses or flip their cups on the table to enjoy a drink. She was amused by their antics but also confused as to how they could drink so much without pairing the alcohol with some form of food. They didn't even snack as they drank. In China, only alcoholics and the homeless could drink on an empty stomach. She continued to stare, wondering what it would be like to have a foreign friend. Surely, they wouldn't be able to communicate well. Their skin colors were completely different, and Ting had always thought that interacting with foreigners would be an impossible task. She wondered how these people managed to get to Shanghai in the first place, considering she was hardly able to survive even a ship ride to Shanghai.

Hua was still outside chatting away. Ting wondered if she had completely forgotten about her. Why invite a person to a place if you're going to spend the entire night on the phone, she thought. As she gazed over to the stage, the band was playing a song that was strange to her ears. It was fast, and the guitar squealed in a wild pitch. The drummer pounded the drums faster than she had ever seen. She watched the singer belt out an anthem that electrified the room. The music was strange, but she liked it. When she glanced back at the table of foreign fools, she noticed that the older, ponytailed man was making his way toward the bar, stopping to chat with some of the other patrons. Ting immediately regretted choosing a seat at the counter, as it was a hotspot for people and she feared to have to speak with anyone that she did not know. The man stumbled over toward the bar once more. He looked directly into Ting's eyes, standing no farther than three feet from her. He continued past and leaned against the bar. The man ordered his drink and then doubled back to pull out the stool next to Ting. It tipped over and crashed to the ground, quickly gathering the attention of the band amidst their performance. The man lifted the chair and dropped himself onto it as he leaned, with one elbow, onto the counter. He looked into Ting's eyes once more, as she leaned slightly away from the man. She could smell the liquor on his breath as he exhaled into her face like a wild boar. His skin looked like glue, only his red nose emerged from the pool of white. He opened his mouth as he stuck out his sticky hands, palms facing inward, hovering in front of his face.

"Hey, you like the big American dicks do ya?"

Ting could not understand the man and she stared at him in sheer terror.

"Hello, I am Ting."

"Ah, *ni hao, ni hao*!"

"Wow, your Chinese is so good!"

"I'm Harry... What is your name?"

"I am fine, thank you."

"No, I mean, what is your *name*?"

"Ting, I am Ting. Sorry, my English is not very well."

"Ting, huh. Do you have a boyfriend, Ting? Have you ever had an *American* boyfriend or you just fuck these Chinese guys? You ever notice they look like chick runway models, their faces are smoother than a baby's ass."

"I do not have a boyfriend."

Ting thought that this was an incredibly personal and direct question to ask. Frankly, she was stunned that the man, Harry, had approached her and spoken to her at all. She could hardly understand what the drunken fool was saying in the first place. This was the first time that she had talked to a foreigner and was weary of using her English since it was the first time in her life that she had used it outside of the classroom. She was in some form of shock, but she was also curious. Ting was not in Huangyan anymore, or what was left of it, at least. She was in an international city and to make it in this town she would have to not only network but learn to talk to people that were different from her. Ting remembered hearing a story of a girl from Huangyan that had made it out and moved to Beijing. She then married a foreigner and had a child with him. The youngster was but two years old before they initiated rather aggressive and emotionally damaging divorce proceedings. The girl had given birth to the child in the month of September and did not leave their apartment until 30 days had passed. Chinese customs often asked new mothers to *zuoyuezi*, which meant that they were not to bathe or leave the apartment for at least a month after giving birth. This would basically leave the woman sitting in her own filth for 30 days straight. Giving birth was an exhausting and painstaking procedure, and women were left vulnerable after birthing a child. Bathing after giving birth left mothers at risk of catching a cold. Stepping outside of the apartment would leave them surrounded by an airborne cloud of diseases that could easily infect and harm their bodies. The British husband considered this custom a comprehensive exhibition of lunacy. He thought it a waste of time and a gross misunderstanding of previously proven medical science. He filed divorce proceedings after concluding that there was no way that he and his wife could ever see eye to eye on even the most basic of cultural and hygienic customs. The residents of Huangyan were in sync with the latest gossip and from there on out would come to label foreign men as deviants and scoundrels. They considered them incapable of ever understanding Chinese culture and the long lineage of traditions that came with it.

Hua returned in time to see Ting speaking with Harry and quickly approached them to introduce herself. Unfortunately, Harry walked away to retrieve his drink and accompany his group before Hua could make her introduction. She immediately proceeded to question Ting about how she knew Harry and upon realizing that Harry had come and introduced himself to her first, she was eager to learn about Ting's specific tactics. Ting couldn't understand what the purpose of the interrogation was, but Hua had been trying for months to meet a foreign man and explained to Ting the immense benefits of potentially achieving success.

"Do you know how easy life becomes once you meet a foreigner and get them to marry?" she asked.

"What do you mean, why would it be easier than usual?"

"Foreign men make a lot of money in China. Sure, there are a lot of rich Chinese guys, but they only choose the most beautiful women, and usually not just one of them."

"That's true. I need stability," said Ting.

"The foreign men don't care about beauty as much as the Chinese. They will marry anyone they think has a kind personality."

"They don't care about beauty?" asked Ting.

"They don't. And the foreigners can easily find jobs in any city in China because their experiences are different from ours, not to mention they are a rare commodity in China. They also make many businesses seem international."

"Ok, I think I understand," replied Ting.

"They also have a different culture and different customs. They do not treat Chinese women as Chinese men sometimes do, like baby-making machines and home cooks. You need to take the chance and marry if you can."

"That man is old. He seemed drunk and smelled like sweat and peanuts."

"Yes, the Westerners are often disgusting. Their snakes travel through many caves, they are too open-minded and friendly, and their bodies grow hair faster than a wet field grows grass. But actually, the low-quality foreigners make for high-quality husbands. If they are fat or a little ugly, they will be unable to cheat on you. It can be a stable life. If they are shy or have few friends, that's also a good sign."

"Ah…"

"If he asks you, just make sure you tell him you're a traditional girl. They always ask, to see whether we are virgins or not. They pursue Chinese girls either way, but will only marry those of us that say we are traditional. These insecure foreigners want to think they're fucking virgins. Little do they know… Oh, and study your English well."

Ting listened to Hua's advice and sat at the bar carefully and meticulously examining her thoughts. Harry was probably nearing 50 and was certainly more than twice Ting's age. The idea of considering him a suitable candidate for marriage disgusted Ting. Hua went back outside of the bar to answer another phone call.

Harry stood up from his seat next to Ricardo and walked back to the bar, stepping into the nearby restroom. The men's bathroom had 10 urinals. Harry chose the one farthest left, though all of them were vacant and available for use. A Chinese man in his mid-30s entered the restroom shortly after him and after examining the availability of the urinals selected the one directly adjacent to Harry's. He unzipped his pants and slowly shifted his eyes towards Harry, lifting and turning his head gradually towards him. He grinned gently and locked his eyes directly with Harry's. He then leaned towards him, as if he was about to divulge a major secret.

"Hello, foreign face!" he shouted at Harry, projecting a foul odor directly into his face.

"Ah! Get the hell out of here, man!" Harry yelled, as he shook his member and escaped from the uncomfortable situation.

When Harry exited the restroom, Ting was still pondering Hua's words carefully. She never expected to even meet a Westerner, let alone begin a romantic relationship with one. Ting had never even had a boyfriend in her life, due to her mother's warning that she would get some form of disease and die if she did so without permission. She was nervous, but this was, in a way, all part of her plan. She always wanted to start a new and better life outside of Huangyan. Harry approached her as he walked from the restroom back to the table where his group was sitting. He asked her for her phone number, although his phone was still dead. She still hadn't purchased a new phone since she left hers aboard the ship, so she took down Harry's number on a wet napkin. She copied it carefully from a crumpled piece of paper he had retrieved from his pocket and unfolded. Harry stumbled away from the bar, forgetting Ting nearly as quickly as he had begun to hit on her. Ting rewrote the number onto a new napkin, placed it in her bag, and turned back to the bar to order a drink. She soon noticed that Hua had been outside on the phone for an awfully long time and upon checking the outside of the bar, Ting realized that Hua was already long gone. She had probably gotten a call from a boy and vanished as quickly as she had answered it.

Ting reentered the bar alone and listened to the band perform until about 12 in the morning before deciding to leave. An hour earlier, she had watched Harry leave with his friends and enter a taxi. Meanwhile, Ting stayed to consider her next steps, given that Hua's advice was one of the most useful and innovative things she had heard in recent days. She left the bar and took a taxi back to the hotel, seeing as she hadn't the slightest idea of where she was. The cabbie drove as Ting gazed through the back window, thinking of the energy of the bar and marveling at the full moon overhead.

CHAPTER TEN

Harry awoke, realizing that he had called in sick the previous night for his first day of work. The rest of his co-workers had done so as well. He figured he wouldn't be the only one dealing with the wrath of the boss, whoever that was. When he checked his phone, he discovered that he had received a text from an unknown number. He soon found out that the message was from a girl named "Ting," though he couldn't remember who she was. After the group had left the Kona Bar, Colleen and Shaniya went to meet with their Chinese boyfriends. The guys subsequently hailed a taxi, and Markin asked the driver to take them to an unusually dark and low-key alley, far from the lights of the city. Markin lovingly referred to the area as "Hooker Street."

When the group arrived, Markin pointed at the dozens of girls standing on the sidewalks outlining the cracked pavement. Harry stood in shock when he realized that these women were all working girls. Some of them were just teenagers. Most of the Chinese considered these women to be nothing but low-class prostitutes. In a country rampant with prostitution- elegant, upscale brothels were often designed discretely inside of hotel buildings to accommodate government officials, policemen, and a variety of wealthy businessmen. The prostitutes that could not establish working relationships with these pink palaces were left to scavenge for money on the dark and grimy hooker streets. They talked to every poor soul that passed by and they could be purchased for as little as 15 dollars each. Markin reached into his front pocket and began to count and arrange his money. He had his eye on the beautiful girl who stood next to two others, chatting away. The girl had bright red hair, a lollipop in her mouth, and a suspicious bulge in her pants. Ricardo and Dean quickly began hitting on the girls, never having been to Hooker Street before. They had no intentions of paying any of the women for sex, though they later did.

The night progressed from there in a rather predictable fashion.

Harry tried to forget. He got to talking with Ting via text and was immediately asked whether he would be interested in meeting to teach her English. Harry instantly put down the phone, ignoring the request, and headed downstairs to see if any of the other teachers were outside at the picnic table again. When he left the building, he could see that Shaniya and Colleen were at the picnic table sharing a bottle of red wine. He was surprised that the table wasn't already covered in beer, seeing as it was sunny again.

"Hey, how are you ladies doing?" he asked.

"We're fine, you? Where did you guys go yesterday after Kona?" said Shaniya.

"We just went to hang out at a barbecue and then got back here. We called it an early night."

"Oh, ok. Have you heard from the guys yet or anything?"

"No, just some girl named Ting. I have no idea who that is, but she wants me to teach her English- for free I'm assuming," said Harry as he rolled his eyes and laughed.

"Is she the Chinese girl that you were talking to at Kona last night? We saw you chatting with her, she looked paralyzed in fear," said Colleen.

"I have no idea."

"That kind of night, huh?"

"Yeah, I guess I'll just ignore her."

"When a girl here asks you to teach her English, it's code for sex," mentioned Shaniya.

"Ok, I'll call her."

"Hah! Ok Harry, good luck," exclaimed Shaniya as she subtly danced and performed an imitation of Harry kissing a woman.

Harry walked to grab some lunch and ended up ordering another bowl of soup noodles. He let the noodles slither down his throat as he picked up his phone and started texting. Harry was an emotional wreck, but he could see the direction in which his future was going. He finally decided to stop pushing against the current. Harry spent every minute of his day either thinking of the past or trying to resist the vices that inevitably brought him so much joy. He asked Ting the standard questions, hoping that she was beautiful, or at least intelligent. He wondered whether she was a student or a worker. He asked her how old she was, to make sure she was of legal age for sexual intercourse. Harry was unaware that the legal age of consent in China was 14. He also asked her if she was a traditional girl, being previously told, by Markin, to do so for every Chinese girl.

Ting texted back in excitement, but she remembered what Hua had told her. If she replied and said that she had a traditional mindset, she would be viewed by Harry as a shy virgin, but she would at least be considered a potential wife. On the other hand, if she replied stating that she was not a traditional girl, she would be viewed as promiscuous, but there would be a higher chance of Harry taking an interest in her. Ting replied to the text message, saying that she was not sure of Harry's meaning, effectively sidestepping the question altogether. Harry moved on and asked Ting out to dinner directly. Afterward, he quickly added to the request, stating that she was the most beautiful girl he had ever seen. Harry still couldn't remember who she was, let alone what she looked like, but thought that these sentiments would convince her to meet with him. He waited, staring at the phone while finishing off a beer. Five minutes passed without a response. After ten minutes, fifteen minutes, and then twenty-five minutes passed, Harry had forgotten that he had even asked Ting out to dinner in the first place. She finally replied, asking when he wanted to go out and meet. Harry suggested meeting the upcoming weekend, and Ting quickly agreed. Ting instantly became nervous and quickly second-guessed her decision, but planned to evaluate all her options before jumping to any extreme conclusions. She kept Hua's words in mind. They planned to set the exact time and location of the date later in the week.

At work, Harry was already showing signs of struggle, having called in sick the very first day. He failed to consider the fact that his co-workers had already accumulated time off during their lengthy contracts, while he hadn't even begun to work. On the second day, he arrived unshaven and unprepared after receiving a brief training from Markin, advising him to "just go in and speak English to the students," because it was just "*that* easy." While the other teachers in the group had collected multimedia presentations and teaching materials from months and years of steady employment there, Harry arrived to class with nothing but an old notebook with some scribblings inside. He read from the notebook and asked students if they had any questions he could answer. Parents soon called the school director to complain about Harry, claiming that their children could smell alcohol on his breath before class. They mentioned that he was not preparing lessons promptly and that he often ended classes early. Surely enough, Harry was fired after his first week of teaching. He had, however, only been hired on a business visa and was technically working illegally, since a work permit was required for legitimate employment. The business visa allowed him to stay in China for periods of three months and required him to exit and reenter the country after each period. This also meant that his visa was not tied to any employer and that he could stay in the country without supervision, given that he followed the rules regarding exiting and reentering.

He left the school after being let go and began walking to his apartment, stopping at the penis liquor store on the way. The shop owner, Ip, couldn't understand what Harry wanted to purchase, despite Harry speaking English at an increasingly high volume. The loud sounds further confused Ip. He ignored the noisy commands and filled three flasks of the good stuff for Harry. Harry continued to the apartment community as he texted Ting, hoping to finally schedule their date.

Ting, on the other hand, had been working steadily at her new job at the Double Happy Good Smoke headquarters. She adapted to office life well, and there was no sweaty factory floor to clean at the headquarters. The stuffing machines that lined the floors of the Huangyan branch were replaced by modern computers and filing cabinets at the Shanghai office. She took great pleasure in pressing the computer keys repeatedly, portraying the appearance of a hard-working employee. She still resided at the hotel, taking a taxi to and from work every day. She was casually looking for an apartment room to rent but was still making enough money to afford the cozy hotel room. She didn't mind the hotel and quickly grew quite fond of it. Ting kept in touch with Hua, messaging her once a day for a brief and often useless dialogue. She was slowly establishing herself in Shanghai but still needed stability. Ting checked her phone eagerly every hour waiting to hear back from Harry.

The following weekend they were finally able to meet. Harry took a taxi from the convenience shop in his apartment community to meet Ting at the "Double Lucky" restaurant. Double Lucky specialized in *huoguo*, hotpot cuisine. Most locals considered hotpot essential to daily life. It was an activity as much as it was a meal and was often set up with a large, round table that contained an electric stove in the center. A huge, boiling cauldron was then placed on the center plate and could heat a variety of soups fairly quickly. The soups ranged from mild to spicy and from sour to sweet, but all were guaranteed to give patrons diarrhea. Across the dining hall, waiters carried a live monkey from the kitchen to the table reserved for the wealthiest guests. This process initiated a rarely-seen event and, by pure coincidence, Harry was present to witness it. The waiters struggled to control the live creature, though the monkey soon conceded to the persistent barbarians. The top of the primate's head had been removed, though the animal was still conscious. Waiters then positioned the unfortunate being under the table until its head was revealed, rising through the hole in the center of the table. A single, dead-eyed, waiter then proceeded to pour boiling soup into the monkey's skull, effectively cooking the brains instantaneously. The guests laughed as the animal screamed, and soon after, became completely silent. This meal was considered an authentic delicacy. The cluster of enthusiastic guests feasted as the ape's blood covered their carnivorous teeth and dripped from their pointed chins.

Just outside of the dining room, patrons watched as Harry stumbled and propelled himself over a raised sidewalk. He propped himself up against the wall of the building, walked in, and sat down at a round table with a single open seat facing the entrance. Harry was never able to maintain his composure or even blend in with a crowd after a few dozen drinks. The dinner party he had joined looked stunned to see him. Several of the older women started to whisper, while their husbands just stared in anticipation. The seat facing the door was reserved for the special guest of the evening. Harry arranged his sweaty frame atop the wooden throne, oblivious to his surroundings. He began to sink into his chair, still completely unaware that he had disrupted the evening for the dinner guests. They had been too shy to cause a commotion, and so Harry sat with his head tilted downwards. His eyelids slowly fell. When the original occupant of the seat returned, Harry felt a tapping on his shoulder that quickly jolted him back into reality. Realizing that he had entered the restaurant and seated himself at the first available place in sight, he stood and began to wobble through the dining room of the restaurant looking for Ting. Many patrons were seated with their families and children, enjoying a weekend evening with their loved ones. They continued to watch in awe as Harry staggered through the narrow paths between the circular tables. Children, who were initially terrified of the sight, began to giggle and even mock Harry. A waitress quickly darted over to Harry and began to carefully escort him to the door. Moments later, Ting appeared from the bathroom hallway. She spotted him and rushed towards the waitress to explain that Harry was her guest. The waitress bowed slightly and scurried away.

Harry sat at the appropriate table and instantly noticed that he was surrounded by Ting and two of her friends. She had invited her new co-workers out to dinner to accompany her. He had been under the impression that he was to meet her for a private dinner, but was unaware of standard Chinese customs that laid out the framework for courting women. Chinese women almost always brought along several of their friends when meeting a man for dinner for the first time. The logic behind this procedure was twofold.

First, it would place the man in an uncomfortable position and therefore build the woman's confidence. This would force a potential suitor to not only impress his date but her friends as well. The situation mostly prompted men to entice the friends into forming romantic feelings of their own. After all, how could they approve of a man that they themselves would not date? The infatuation that subsequently developed within the friends of these women often primed the runways for the affairs that later ensued. These sidekick friends thrived on the luxuries of living as mistresses. They shared the spoils of war with the wives and reached deep into the pockets of their lovers. But unlike the wives, they were not expected to reproduce with the men.

Secondly, this custom brought women peace of mind, as they could not be easily raped by strangers while in the company of their friends.

Considering Harry was too drunk to even sit up, he quickly got over the realization that he was to be put on trial by these judgmental succubae. Harry's head was spinning, but he was no longer nervous to resume his dating lifestyle. He peered into the smoldering pot of broth at the center of the table and dipped his spoon inside to taste it. The girls giggled and proceeded to place raw meat and vegetables into the soup. They would be boiled in the broth and ready for consumption within minutes. The tasteless treats could then be dipped into a sesame paste sauce and consumed.

"So, Harry, you are a teacher? So cool!" exclaimed one of Ting's co-workers.

"Yeah, I'm a teacher alright. What about you ladies?"

"How much money do you make?" asked another.

"Well, actually, I was just fired from my job," he replied.

"I see," said the prodding viper.

Ting slouched into her chair.

"Your nose is so big. You are very handsome!" blurted the excited one.

"Do you have a girlfriend? How old are you? How long do you plan to stay in China? Do you like Chinese girls?" asked the viper, in a fury of impatience.

Harry choked on the dreadful black liquor dripping from his flask. He was caught off guard by her intense and provoking personal questions.

"I thought I was going to dinner alone with Ting, so why the hell would I have a girlfriend?"

The girls were quickly silenced. They looked at each other calmly and changed the subject immediately. One of them pulled up a web page on her phone and began showing off her latest online purchases. Harry couldn't bear the conversation any longer and considered the ghastly stew in the center of the table to be repulsive. He excused himself from the setting to use the restroom, knocking over a glass of tea that spilled all over the wooden table as he rose. Harry walked through the doors of the restaurant, tossed an empty flask into the busy road, and entered another liquor store. He picked up two more bottles and hailed a taxi, showing the driver the directions to Hooker Street that Markin had previously given him. Ting and her co-workers were still at the restaurant and had watched as Harry boldly walked through the exit doors.

"Do you think he is the best choice for you Ting?" asked the viper, giving her direct opinion of Harry as indirectly as she possibly could.

"I think he's cute enough!" replied the overzealous friend.

"Cute enough?" asked the viper, rhetorically, as she leaned in closer.

"He is disgusting! Did you notice his smell? He was obviously drunk. Harry is much too old for you, Ting. He should trade his ponytail in for a job, he's broke!"

Ting was lost in a deep state of thought. She was initially excited to have roped a potentially prestigious man into her life but was now having serious second thoughts. The girls ate together, dipping various meats into the sesame goo. The viper would continue to comment on the situation at three-minute intervals, but Ting remained silent in contemplation and waited for the tyrant's berating to conclude. The viper paid the bill, and the girls left the restaurant around ten o'clock. They took the stairs, as the elevator had dropped and cut someone in half just hours ago, and was shut down for maintenance. The girls watched as two coroners carefully dragged heavy black bags through the bloody rubble. Ting parted ways with the girls and decided to walk back to the hotel alone. She walked along the dark, cracked sidewalks, stepping around the sinkholes that seemed to lurk within them. Ting hardly knew Harry, and so she could hardly make the decision to abstain from seeing him in the future. Then again, she barely knew her new co-workers. Perhaps the viper was planting doubt in her mind so that she could steal Harry for herself later on.

Ting scoffed and continued onwards, crossing the street in the direction of the hotel. She was proceeding on another dimly-lit sidewalk when she heard a nearly inaudible wailing from an even gloomier alleyway. Ting entered, noticing a young girl, about nine years old, lying next to a dumpster and clenching her leg. Hours earlier, the girl had been hit by a garbage truck. The driver continued on his route without so much as slowing after plowing through the girl. At the time, the alley was well lit and populated, though not a single soul came to her rescue. Security footage would later show that over 200 people had passed by the girl, without even one stopping to lend a hand. This may have been due to the lingering ghosts of certain Chinese laws that transferred the full responsibility for an injured person's health to the person assisting them. If anyone had stopped to help the girl, they would be at risk. If the girl later died, the good Samaritan would be responsible and thus punished with either a life sentence or a 40-hour walloping with a sack of potatoes. The specific punishment would be chosen at the judge's discretion. As Ting approached the girl, she noticed that the girl was in terrible pain. Realizing this, she ran from the girl as fast as she could. She was terrified that she would be held liable. She turned the corner of the alley and dialed for the ambulance to come. She then continued on her way. Ting had already done more than most would ever consider doing for a person in a similar situation. She soon returned to the hotel, and thought about Harry. Ting waited for a message from him, to no avail. If she had known that Harry was descending into an endless pit of prostitutes and liver damage, she might have reconsidered her deep infatuation with him. Ting looked through the window once more with anticipation and then slowly closed her eyes.

CHAPTER ELEVEN

In the following weeks, Harry continued to descend into the dark abyss of his own mind. Consistently in a hungover state, pollution and cigarettes soon became familiar odors to him. He was jobless and surviving on his meager savings. They were nearly depleted after having been used to cover his rent payments after his sudden termination from the Happy Family English School. He was now responsible for paying all fees out of pocket. Harry drank until he couldn't feel the pains of his failures, the list of which was growing longer by the day. He drank to the point of involuntary urination. He was hopelessly fucked. Often, his hands shook nervously. His former co-workers had unintentionally limited contact with him. They still needed to work and often went out together immediately after quitting time.

Harry couldn't make it through an entire day in a state of sobriety to meet with them. Instead, he ate soup noodles and drank heavily, retreating to his apartment every afternoon to sleep through the day and begin again at night. Harry frequented Hooker Street and a variety of other brothels, occasionally being forced out for acting aggressively and belligerently drunk. There were nearly two months left on his business visa, at which point he would need to exit and reenter the country to renew the document and add another three months of validity. Harry did not have the funds to even fly to Hong Kong and back to comply with this immigration law.

His derelict apartment was decomposing almost as quickly as his brain cells were shriveling. Harry sat at his window, holding a bottle of cheap serpent wine. This was a rare tonic, made by throwing an adolescent snake into a bottle of poisonous liquor. After months of fermentation, the liquid would be ready for consumption. Looking out the window, he could see that for some people, life was still beautiful. Children still played, couples still held hands and kissed, and the sun still came out from behind the polluted sky from time to time. Harry, on the other hand, had nothing. His job prospects were gone, he did not have any genuine friends in Shanghai, and his family was thousands of miles away. His eyes started to leak as the sun rapidly retreated behind dark, ominous clouds. Black, murky rain began to fall on the streets of Shanghai. He threw his empty flask at the window, shattering it against the metal bars that laid across the glass. Theses bars were quite useful for both deterring intruders and trapping tenants in the event of a fire since they did not allow for even a flask to pass through their defenses.

As Harry sat alone at the table outside of his apartment building, drinking and swaying with the wind, a young foreign man approached to introduce himself. Harry was soaked and tinted black from the murky water that had been falling on his oily hair. The man's name was Markham, and he approached Harry confidently, quickly revealing his face that hid behind his black umbrella. He had been living in China for five years and was now living alone after marrying and soon after abandoning a Russian woman he had met in Shanghai years earlier. Markham's wife was now living with his parents in North Carolina and taking care of their twin children. He had shamelessly banished her to resume his uninhibited lifestyle in Shanghai, but she held no objections as her immigration status was rather favorable in the states. When Harry asked Markham what the purpose of his stay in Shanghai was, he received vague answers. One day Markham would mention that he was studying in China while the next he would divulge that he was there to sell hacked computer game files to Chinese companies. He did this in China to remain far out of reach of American copyright laws.

Markham quickly befriended Harry, and the two drank from morning until night. Markham would take Harry to a variety of bars and clubs. He often claimed that he had connections at these venues with various promoters and managers and that they would be able to drink for free. Harry soon realized that this was a fabrication of Markham's mind. When they arrived at these nightclubs, he would often join a table of complete strangers and begin pouring drinks for everyone, including himself and Harry. The guests were too polite and shy to send him back on his way, and some were even excited to spend time with a potential foreign friend. Their nights would often end with forceful ejection from the clubs or the need to flee from a group of aggressive Chinese men. The two would frequent the hooker streets, brothels, gambling dens, and underground rock shows to distract themselves from a sad reality. Markham thrived on the adrenaline and often considered himself to be exceptionally outgoing, able to get along with anyone while reaping the benefits of his friendships almost instantly. For Harry, this lifestyle was a temporary solution to a much more severe problem. He had been blacking out much more often than ever before, and depression sank deeper into the corners of his mind. He thought about finding a way out every day but continued to fall further into despair.

Meanwhile, Ting was climbing the ranks of her company headquarters. She was promoted to full-time assistant manager and had secured a bedroom for herself in an apartment just outside of the city center. She sometimes considered the fate of Huangyan and her friends who resided there, but they were in the past, and she was hellbent on looking toward the future. She was doing well but was quickly growing tired of work altogether. Ting saw pampered women that drove their husbands' expensive cars, and she would gaze in awe. These vixens strutted throughout the streets, draped in mink coats, and reflected walnut-sized diamonds into

Ting's eyes. This filled her with a kind of dormant jealousy. She wondered how these women could live such lifestyles without working a single minute of the day. She resented them and expanded her goals once more, after all, why should they be the only ones to enjoy these luxuries?

Ting had been spending time with Hua on a few occasions every week. Hua had found an Australian boyfriend who was employed for Shanghai's Public Light and Fencing Department. She regularly boasted that the simple life was just months away as her lover was particularly horrid and sure to marry her soon. His portly figure and obnoxious demeanor would certainly keep other admirers at a distance until she could entrap him in a life of seclusion. Ting thought of Harry right away. She sent him a message asking whether he would be able to join her on a second date, adding that they could go to a more secluded venue to avoid becoming lost in the confusion of a crowded environment. Her statement was worded very carefully to lessen the blame of Harry abandoning their previous dinner at the hotpot restaurant. Ting sat in her cubicle, pretending to type away at the keyboard, and eagerly waited for Harry's response. She imagined walking down the streets of Shanghai with diamonds of her own, purchased by her very own foreign monkey. She smiled and continued to strike her keyboard erratically.

Harry was coming home from a particularly destructive bender when he received Ting's message. He was returning from a night of exploring the city's most obscure corners. He and Markham had been involved in an altercation that left the two beaten and bloodied by a group of motorcyclists in front of Shanghai's "Devil's Den," home to a group of notoriously brutal Chinese bikers. Harry's clock was close to striking midnight, but he quickly replied to Ting's message. Though she had boldly invited him to dinner for the upcoming weekend, he responded by inviting her to his apartment immediately. She read the response several times before completely understanding his request.

Ting (+86 1004455041): You want me to come to your apartment now?

Harry (+86 4440532444): Yeh com over.. and we can watch a movi herer and have a couple some of drink.

Ting (+86 1004455041): I think it is too late now. Maybe another time is better.

Harry (+86 4440532444): Its nut late for a Saterdaiy come ove and we can relax with a couplea drinks Don worry.

Ting was understandably confused as to the meaning of Harry's message, quickly identifying that he thought it was Saturday rather than Friday. She ignored the mistake and considered his proposition. Ting was incredibly nervous to meet Harry at his apartment after only having previously met him once in her life. She often heard about foreign, white ghosts and their infamous enjoyment of the *yiyeqing*. She couldn't understand how people could meet only once and participate in sexual intercourse. For Ting, who had never had a boyfriend let alone intercourse, a one night stand was more of a distant fantasy than a real possibility. She was anxious, but she did not want to miss out on the opportunity to connect with Harry and secure his attention. She agreed to come over on the condition that they were to spend time together in a friendly manner. Ting did not want to sleep with Harry, who was really still a stranger to her. Harry gave her his address and immediately faded away, passing out on the floor of the kitchen after leaning against his refrigerator and pouring another drink. By the time Ting arrived, he was already compiling a pile of drool next to his face. He flung open his eyelids and sat up, listening for the door again to make sure the sound was not a mere figment of his imagination. As Ting knocked again, Harry stood up, wondering who could be knocking at his door this late in the evening. He opened the door and upon realizing it was Ting, invited her to come inside.

"What movie do you want to watch?" she asked, innocently.

"I don't, I don't know, I may have a couple of movies on my laptop. Whadda ya want to drink?"

"Do you have any comedies?"

"Yeah, I think so. You like rum, right?" Harry asked, giving Ting a glass filled to the brim with three-penis wine.

Ting couldn't possibly drink the liquor straight but sipped from the cup to keep from inconveniencing Harry. Meanwhile, Harry downed another two glasses of the toxic sludge and placed his laptop on the coffee table in front of his bed. The bed was bare, without bedsheets or covers. Harry had pulled it into the living room. This gave him peace and helped him fall asleep to the sounds of the city. Ting sat on the bed reluctantly to get a good view of the movie. She slid her body over to the edge of the bed, avoiding the mysterious stains that had situated themselves within the fabric.

"I have not asked you yet, where are you from?" she asked.

"I'm from the states."

"Oh, I very like New York."

"Yeah, that's a good spot."

"Does your family live in New York? Do they have a big house and a backyard?"

"No, they don't live there. My family's spread out all over the states. My brothers have families and houses and bills and responsibilities now."

She finished her drink and began to feel dizzy. She excused herself to use the restroom and stood on the battered tiles, staring at the mirror and trying to compose herself. When she returned, Harry was waiting for her under the covers that he had retrieved while she was away. He told her that she could lie back and relax so that she could enjoy the movie. He played a download of an old 80s comedy on the laptop's bright display. Ting sat on the bed, atop the covers, with her back upright and legs crossed, placing her empty glass on the nightstand. Harry crawled out from beneath the covers, grabbed her drink, and refilled it in the kitchen. When he came back to the living room, Ting was already texting on her phone, ready to concoct an excuse to leave the apartment and return home. She felt uncomfortable sitting on Harry's bed alone, and she could not trust him. She feared that she would hardly be able to trust herself. Ting knew that Harry had a drinking problem, judging by the speed at which he devoured his drinks. She wanted to go home and forget all about her plan to marry a foreigner. She would settle for a wealthy Chinese man and never think of this day again.

Harry handed her the glass, and she drank from it halfheartedly. He soon slid back under the covers of the bed and invited her to join him. She thought she was going to have a panic attack. Ting didn't want to be considered promiscuous, but she also did not want to become a left-behind girl. This concern of hers was, of course, of the idea that any girl who was unmarried and single by age 26 was to be left to suffer the fate of a lonely spinster. Women that were unable to secure a suitable mate by that age were certainly defective and incapable of completing even the most basic functions of a human female. She would be unable to procreate and serve her purpose in China's traditional society. This worried her as she was only a few years away from the cut-off point. She slowly crawled under the bedsheets. Ting immediately became aware that Harry had already disrobed. His genitalia gently brushed against her left leg as he proceeded to unclothe her.

"Is everything OK? I'm not really getting any feedback here."

"I am OK," she replied.

He proceeded to undress her and clumsily mounted her. She braced for impact as the wildebeest thrust himself inside of her. She felt pain, but she was also becoming excited. She was enduring a main component of a healthy relationship, or so she had often been told. Harry continued to propel himself into the girl and quietly belched while they fornicated. His sweat fell on her smooth back as she winced from the sensation. She thought of the strangeness of repeatedly ramming an appendage into a female vagina for pleasure. Ting felt ashamed, but she also felt aroused. She could not openly portray this feeling, for fear of being categorized as an "open-minded woman." She laid there, like a dead fish, waiting for Harry to finish his business while holding back conflicted cries of joy. He flipped and turned her like a butcher. As Harry concluded his vigorous panting atop the delicate girl, he collapsed onto the bed, beside Ting. She laid quietly, enduring the moderate pain and discomfort of losing her virginity. She rested motionlessly for several minutes, evaluating what had occurred and proceeded to run every possible scenario through her head. She wondered what the next step in their relationship would be and pondered whether he would now propose to her right away or whether he would plan to do so on special occasion. Ting couldn't help but also wonder how Harry had gotten her to sleep with him so quickly. She speculated that he had probably done so with many other girls and she immediately became apprehensive about her decision to give herself to him. As Harry stood and entered the bathroom, she became paranoid and began to search his bed for stray hairs. Her friends in Huangyan had always told her that in the event of a one-night stand with a handsome Chinese man, she would need to search their beds for strands of hair that could belong to previous lovers. Ting scanned every inch of his bed in pursuit of these stray hairs, avoiding the small patches of blood she had produced. She was hoping to determine whether Harry was a potential husband or just another foreign playboy. She found a single, black strand, but soon realized that, in all likelihood, it was her own. She felt relieved and was once again determined to capitalize on this opportunity to forever secure Harry's love.

When Harry returned from the restroom, Ting smiled at him lovingly. She curled up next to him on the bed and kissed his cheek as she gripped him tighter. Ting imagined all the ways in which Harry would show his love to her. Ting also began to dream of all the apartments they would own, all the cars that Harry would later buy her, and all the children that she would give to him. In her mind, this would be an even trade. Even though Harry had recently fallen on hard times, Ting believed that there was great potential to unlock within him and that the relationship would certainly pay off in the end. She also thought of Hua and smirked at the thought of hearing about her new lover. Hua would undoubtedly be jealous upon first seeing them together. Everything was going according to plan for Ting. Her employment was stable and secure, her rented room in the apartment was beautiful, and she had a serious prospect for marriage. Harry looked down at her, and she clenched his arm within her tiny hands. He looked back up and coughed, swallowing a rather repulsive portion of phlegm. There were a couple of habits that she would seek to change in Harry, she thought.

Harry sat up, still naked on his bed, and glanced at Ting.

"You're on the pill, right?" he asked.

"What is 'pill'?" she asked in return.

Ting had not been aware of the meaning of the word, but she had also not been aware of the existence of such contraceptives. Unfortunately, she was not on "the pill" and was stunned to learn, from Harry, about the apparently common use of the medication. Harry had been too drunk and careless to employ protective measures before intercourse and upon his realization of this, was hoping that Ting was at least equipped with some sort of protection of her own. Growing up in China, and especially within a more rural section of the country, she had never received any form of sex education from her public-school teachers. The subject was considered taboo, and although there was a portion of every science curriculum set aside to cover it, most teachers refrained from doing so to prevent awkward and uncomfortable situations in the classroom.

Parents did not require the teachers to educate their children on these subjects as they were never taught themselves. The idea of their children having sex had also been banished from their minds. The use of contraception was unnecessary as they did not plan for their children to have sexual relations until after marriage. After all, to them, the entire purpose of sex was to create life. Ting quickly disregarded any worry in regards to this topic, as her plan was to procreate anyway. She assumed that since Harry had initiated a romantic relationship with her, that was his plan as well. Harry soon forgot all about the dilemma and dozed off, inebriated and exhausted.

As the sun rose, Ting awoke, once again hopeful of what the day would bring. She peered at Harry as he slept, completely exposed and unconscious. His body was misshapen. Sweat evaporated, and the stench of liquor emanated from his skin. Reddish-brown hair covered his figureless body and reflected the sun's light into Ting's eyes. She could hear his heart beating. She hoped that it would beat for the rest of her life. As she lowered her eyes, she realized that his pink penis was completely exposed as well. She gasped at the sight. She hadn't seen much of the events of the night before. The lights were off, and the apartment was pitch black at the time. Ting stared at him in a great curiosity that was paired with mild revulsion. When he awoke, he was surprised to find Ting in his bed. Harry was also initially surprised to find himself naked but had accustomed himself to accepting these strange and frequent occurrences. He cooked a bowl of packaged noodles for Ting and quickly sent her on her way, saying that he needed to get ready and prepare for several job interviews later in the day. This was, of course, a blatant lie, and Ting knew it was unlikely. She disregarded his reasoning for wanting her to leave and assumed that he was acting politely since he at least offered a reason. This was common practice in China and friends often lied to each other in such ways. He needed to get her out of his apartment as soon as possible. He felt more comfortable drunk and alone than with a total stranger. She happily took off down the stairs with the satisfaction of having successfully reformed the man. Ting could already see that by being with her, Harry was becoming more courteous. He had cooked breakfast for her and had possibly even acquired the determination to find another job. She assumed that he wanted to please her. Ting stepped outside and hailed a cab. Harry watched her from his window, poured himself another drink and lit a cigarette.

CHAPTER TWELVE

A couple of weeks passed as Harry and Ting's lives remained uneventful. Harry continued with his drinking. By this point, the pain of his divorce had all but left his shallow heart. It had been drowned out by the hundreds of liters of effective poisons he had been medicating himself with. He had all but given up, yet Ting continued to message and call him daily. She would arrive at his apartment unannounced bearing food, gifts, and clothing. For Ting, these were the ways that she could show her love for him. For Harry, these treats were often unexpected, but well received. He couldn't understand why she kept appearing with them, but regardless, his love for her did grow to some extent. She imagined reforming the sloppy specimen of a man that Harry had become, thus solidifying his love for her. And Harry did begin to love her, but he did so reluctantly and with ulterior motives in mind. He believed that if his life were to continue as it had been, spending 16 hours of the day drinking and toiling away in the slums of Shanghai with Markham, he would encounter an inevitable, ominous fate. Harry knew that his worn, elderly body could not sustain itself much longer under these conditions and that he needed a strong woman to reform him. He saw that Ting loved him boundlessly and he often gave in to her demands, accepting her requests for him to shower and even change his clothing from time to time.

Ting utilized every opportunity to leave her mark on Harry. She would come over to his apartment and wait for him to use the restroom, as he often did predictably after becoming intoxicated. She would then scroll through his phone, deleting dozens of contacts whose names appeared to be female. Ting still rifled the bed for strands of hair but never found any evidence to incriminate Harry. She left toothbrushes and hairpins scattered throughout his apartment to deter any potential lovers from coming back. Ting was a jealous woman. She had given herself to Harry in a moment of lust and desire and now wanted to be the sole possessor of his affection. Ting would ensure that her sacrifices would pay off in this investment. She told her grandparents about her circumstances, withholding nearly every critical detail of the situation. Ting told them that she had met a delightful, rich man and that she wanted to bring him to Huangyan to show him around the small city. She neglected to tell them that he was her boyfriend, but that announcement would come in due time. The excitement of bringing Harry to meet her family was overwhelming. Ting's grandparents had been residing in her parents' home since their untimely deaths. They sat in the kitchen throughout all hours of the day, snacking and playing cards. They listened to the radio and occasionally shouted back at the host through the speakers, projecting bits of rice across the room from their toothless mouths. Ting's grandparents were essentially indifferent to their granddaughter's current hopes and dreams. They still blamed her for the death of her parents and listed a variety of events that they felt were Ting's responsibility like neglecting to teach her mother to use the phone without being thrown through the car's windshield. They reluctantly agreed to meet Harry, though they decided to only let him stay with them for one night.

Ting asked Harry to accompany her to her hometown, explaining to him that her friends were throwing a small party at a KTV and that he would be able to get to know her better if he saw where she had come from. Days before, Ting had contacted her friends that were still back in Huangyan. She became aware that DanDan was still alive, while many of her other friends had perished in the factory explosion several months earlier. DanDan was especially upset to learn of the fact that Ting had left the city without so much as a goodbye. She also grew envious that Ting was living in Shanghai and working as an assistant manager in the factory's headquarters. DanDan felt more experienced and better qualified than Ting, especially considering the age gap between them. As the older of the two, DanDan felt that she should be wealthier and better off than her best friend. She would likely hold on to this subtle resentment for the rest of her life but temporarily made peace with Ting as most of her other friends were now deceased. Ting informed DanDan and her few remaining friends that she had found a foreign boyfriend and future husband, but told her grandparents that she was bringing a friend and potential business partner to town. As far as they knew,

Harry was coming to the city to establish *guanxi* and formulate new business relationships. Ting's friends were excited to meet the foreign man that had stolen her heart.

Ting notified Harry that they would be leaving for Huangyan the next morning. He agreed to go. Harry had always wanted to travel throughout China but had gotten caught up in the cyclical periods of inebriation that often befell expats abroad. She told him that she would prepare the tickets for their voyage and that all Harry needed to bring was a small piece of luggage with a couple days' worth of clothing. He would stay with Ting and her grandparents but would be required to sleep on the couch in the living room. This would prevent the two from staying awake late at night and possibly kissing. Harry thought this was excessive considering the two had already participated in drunken, unprotected sex the first night in his apartment.

When he hung up the phone, he vomited into his kitchen sink and collapsed on the cold floor. Panic overtook his frail body. He needed to go to the hospital, but help was out of reach. Harry's neighbors could not speak English and would never consider coming to the aid of a stranger's cries for help. He struggled to crawl out of the kitchen to make it to the main door in the living room. This time, he felt as though he may have finally done it. His fingers and hands began to tingle as his legs went numb. He could feel his throat closing as his eyelids struggled to keep from shutting. As he crawled through piles of his own bile, Harry felt that his body may finally resign. His heart beat faster, and his movement slowed. He laid on his stomach and closed his eyes, preparing for the end. He faded away once more into the twilight of the evening.

Ting arrived at Harry's apartment early the next morning. Her luggage was packed and waiting for her at the bottom of the building's old, dusty staircase. She knocked on the door and received nothing but silence in return. She checked her new phone for the time, confirming that she had arrived at the correct hour. Ting knocked once more and waited for a response, but once again, total silence ensued. She began to worry that Harry would not be ready in time. Tardiness was an unpleasant trait of the man, and she had hoped to leave in the past. This was not to mention that if they missed their flight, Ting's airline coupon would be rendered invalid.

Ting also came bearing great news about her employment status. Earlier in the morning, she had spoken on the phone with the owner of Shanghai's Double Happy Good Smoke. Her manager offered Ting a promotion and asked her to stay home throughout the early hours of the morning to receive an express letter delivery. She had been promoted to the International Franchise Division of the company as a certified agent. This would allow her the privilege of traveling extensively in the future. The promotion also offered her paid days off, and she immediately used her first one. This way she could be paid for the two days she was about to spend traveling with Harry. Ting was excited to give Harry the news.

She tried to peer through the door's peephole, and an angered frown overcame her face. She knocked for the last time before gradually pushing his door open to peer inside. Harry was lying on the floor just feet from the entrance. She rushed to his motionless body and began to shake and pull at his shirt, trying to awaken him. Ting quickly considered leaving the apartment and forgetting the man altogether but had grown to seriously love him. She considered dialing 120 for medical assistance but knew that the ambulance would likely arrive hours later. Ting turned his body over as the whites of his eyes slowly appeared. He gasped deeply as he rapidly jerked himself awake. Harry's eyes were bloodshot, and his skin had been releasing alcohol through its pores throughout the night. He looked at Ting as if surprised to see her, and immediately realized he had promised to travel to Huangyan with her. She helped him stand and quietly cleaned him up in the restroom. Not a word escaped her mouth. She was distressed from the situation and unable to communicate her feelings to Harry at that moment. Ting polished him down to a presentable appearance and brought him outside to hail a taxi to the airport. Harry sat in the back seat, panting and dry-heaving, trying not to vomit onto the carpeted floors. Ting sat, watching the city through the window, reconsidering her decision to reform and invest in this man. After all, she was doing extremely well at the Huangyan Double Happy Good Smoke headquarters. As a new international franchise agent, she would be receiving not only a higher salary but commissions as well. Conducting business within China would leave her with a considerable profit, despite 80 percent of gross earnings being allocated toward bribing local officials and overweight government officers. If she decided to conduct business abroad, she would also be left with considerable profit, with only 75 percent of gross earnings needing to be allocated toward various socialist taxes. Ting looked back at Harry, who had fallen asleep with his face pressed against the cab's dirty window. She then reached into her purse and glanced at the yellow express envelope she received in the mail from her manager just hours earlier. She clenched the envelope and turned to look back through the window.

CHAPTER THIRTEEN

By the time that Ting and Harry had boarded the plane and arrived in Huangyan, Harry was sober. He was exhausted, but he could walk upright and respond to questions in a rational manner, though he stayed relatively silent. Ting walked through the glass doors of the airport and looked around in awe. This was the first time she had returned to Huangyan in nearly three months. It appeared as though the city had become more polluted during the time that Ting had been in Shanghai. She looked at the grayish smog of Huangyan in disgust. The city was below her now. After all, she was a city girl with a more dignified job than most of her old high school friends. She was the one that had made it out entirely on her own, with nothing in her pockets except half of Captain Lang's life savings. Ting hardly missed Huangyan, but a feeling of nostalgia overcame her nonetheless. She hailed a cab once again, and the two sat in the back as Ting directed the driver to her home.

Harry was nauseous but finally aware of his surroundings. He looked in wonder at the small city, but also immediately noticed the extreme pollution in the air. The presence of state-operated factories was often the cause of the toxic air, with the local government requiring a certain amount of production from each of the enormous sweatshops within city limits. The decreasing temperatures and gradual arrival of winter also forced cities to engage heating systems powered by the burning of coal. As the fuel burned to keep buildings and residents warm, particulates lingered in the air for days. Near the airport, fog covered buildings in a blanket of bright gray haze. Ting and Harry could hardly distinguish buildings that were but 100 meters away. The air had a taste that was instantly recognizable to Ting, but strange and uncomfortable to Harry. He could feel the metallic dust on his tongue while the taxi's heater blew the fog down his nostrils. The smoke quickly dried his throat. Huangyan officials were limited in their options to dissipate the airborne toxins. Citizens could wait for natural rainfall that would cause black water drops to fall upon the city. They could also wait for heavy winds that would carry the toxic fumes to another nearby town. Lastly, they could temporarily disengage factory production. Local officials would hardly ever order a stop to factory production and much preferred a slight increase in lung cancer reports. They only halted production when a televised event was being held in Huangyan, to give the appearance of a clean and healthy city. When pharmaceutical factories spewed ghastly contaminants, city officials proudly claimed that the fumes were beneficial to citizens since they were medicines that were being released into the air free of charge. Harry looked at the concrete factories that endlessly lined the highway, each releasing their own distinct shade of gray mist. He was amazed that people could survive under these conditions at all. The truth was that the locals could hardly notice the air quality of the city anymore. Most of the residents grew accustomed to the haze from a very young age, despite the pollution being most harmful to humans in their earliest years. They adapted in ways that would surprise any outsider. Their lungs were mutated, causing them to instantly become ill when traveling in cleaner, less polluted cities. Growing up in the pollution directly caused this irreversible damage to young and developing lungs. Many children would grow up knowing that they would never even make it to their 40s.

When Ting and Harry arrived at Ting's childhood home, Harry was nervous to meet her grandparents. He excused himself even before entering the home, stating that he needed to stop by the convenience store to buy a shaving razor and cream so that he could be more presentable to them. Ting warned Harry that it would be unwise to drink alcohol. She mentioned that her grandparents would surely notice and disapprove of such a careless man. Harry turned and started walking toward the store. When he returned to the house, he entered without knocking and without removing his shoes. Ting was already sitting at the kitchen table catching up with her grandparents when he stumbled in. Her grandparents' eyes widened as they noticed this massive, white minotaur, barreling towards them. They understood that they needed to show respect to the man. He was a potential business partner of Ting's, but they could not contain their looks of awe. Harry introduced himself as he shook hands with her grandfather, squeezing the life out of his fingers while slapping the old man's shoulder. The bones within the man's hand crackled, and he quickly pulled back his shriveled extremities. He kissed Ting's grandmother on the cheek and hugged her, leaning his weight against her. These greetings were especially strange for the couple, considering that firm handshakes were often considered aggressive and kissing, regardless of intent, was reserved only for loved ones in private. Harry released her from his grasp and stumbled backward, leaning against the refrigerator. His hand slipped on the slick, metallic surface and he fell into the hard counter, violently cursing under his breath.

Ting's grandparents were stunned by this display of drunkenness, but they had not had company in months and were rather amused by Harry's ridiculous antics. Harry began to rifle through their cabinets as Ting cringed. She wondered how she could ever tell them that Harry was indeed her boyfriend. His drinking problem had grown beyond repair, she thought. He was out of control. At a certain point, she would have to abandon the sinking ship that their relationship was on, but it was emotionally difficult for her to do so. Harry pulled out four glasses from the cabinet and started to fill them with the liquor he had purchased from the convenience store down the street. Within minutes he had convinced Ting's grandparents to drink with him, purely by gesturing like a mentally ill baboon. The old man started to enjoy Harry's company. Not only was he amused by his strange demeanor, but he admired how open and outgoing these foreign beasts were. They had become friends incredibly quickly. Ting's grandmother came to have a slight crush on Harry and wondered what his bare, ghostly body would look like. She imagined the things he would do to her if she were only 50 years younger. Ting remained conflicted since her opinion of Harry seemed to change with every ongoing moment. She was proud to have found such potential in this ungroomed monster, but often, she saw no hope in his improvement. Ting had begun to love him as she spent more time with him, but the thought of him spending time with her merely due to his altered perception often worried her. She understood that his alcoholism was a serious concern, but as she did not see Harry every day of the week, she was unaware of just how serious his problem had become. Ting's grandpa headed to the bedroom to ready his accordion as Harry began dancing in the kitchen, slamming into walls and knocking items from the counter. Everyone but Ting, who had only downed a couple of shots, was too drunk to notice by this point. The night grew late as the four bonded through the evening, drinking and singing songs from their home countries.

The next morning, Ting and Harry awoke, in separate rooms, and met in the kitchen for breakfast prepared of steamed buns and boiling hot soy milk. Her grandparents were still in a deep slumber after the previous night's festivities. Ting walked into the bathroom feeling unexpectedly queasy, and she assumed the feeling was a result of the activities from the previous evening. She quickly kneeled and vomited into the toilet. In the kitchen, Harry gagged at the scent and texture of the tasteless snacks, meant to merely fill the stomach as any basic piece of cardboard would similarly do. Harry had grown tired of noodles, and other vile foods often sold on the streets by vendors that clearly neglected to take hygiene and proper food preparation into consideration. The street food that he had encountered up to this point had evacuated a lifetime of bowels in just a few short months. He could see that the food in Ting's home was clean, but it tasted like a rolled-up, wet sock. Harry ate the bland, rubber balls and went into the bathroom to swallow it all down with a flask of seahorse wine.

Ting called to him and informed him that DanDan and a few other friends had changed the venue for the day. They would need to leave and meet them at DanDan's hotel room later in the evening. The truth was that Ting had something much more devious planned than a simple night out with her childhood friends. She brought along with her an expensive item that she had recently purchased from one of Shanghai's best jewelers. Ting had identified a gorgeous diamond ring that she selected and fitted perfectly to her left ring finger. She worked on devising a plan to get Harry to give her this ring and had finally formulated a way to do so smoothly. DanDan had booked a one-night stay at one of Huangyan's most luxurious 3-star hotels. She and her old friends from the factory were able to pool their funds together and schedule a surprise party for Ting and Harry, though the initial idea belonged to Ting. DanDan's goal was to celebrate Ting's new relationship, though in doing so, her own ulterior motives would be revealed. Ting's goal was to make use of her newly acquired diamond ring.

As Ting and Harry arrived and entered the hotel suite, they could see that the room was well decorated. A large television was powered on, with local news broadcasting on the bright screen. The reporter spoke of the dangers in America, stating that everyone in the country was armed with guns and that citizens were killing each other every day. A pie chart appeared next to the reporter showing current American demographics. The diagram exhibited that 99% of Americans were black, while only 1% were of European decent. Ting reached into her purse and gripped a small black box. She hugged Harry warmly, for all to see, and discretely slid the box into one of his cargo pockets. The box subtly rattled against one of the bottles in his pocket. Harry went to the restroom to finish off a couple of flasks he had been working on. The next drink of choice for the evening was, once again, snake wine. He yanked his arm from his pocket suddenly, and his heart seemed to skip a beat. It quickly sent a sharp, needle-like pain through his body. Harry fell to his knees, quickly raising his last flask to avoid spilling even a single drop. He fell over on his side, and the small bottles in his cargo pockets shattered, piercing his thighs.

Meanwhile, Ting and DanDan had been catching up. Ting now saw herself as a wealthy city girl, while DanDan attempted to put her seniority back on display for Ting. The two spoke in a passive-aggressive tone for nearly half an hour, proudly boasting of their recent achievements.

"I've found another job downtown. The money is good for a city like Huangyan. You'll be able to find something like that soon," said DanDan.

"Actually, my job pays very well. I've been promoted to 'Certified Agent' in the International Franchise Department of the Double Happy Good Smoke headquarters in Shanghai," Ting replied.

"It must be very tedious work. You must get so tired living in a big city, it's not peaceful."

"No, it's exciting. The work will allow me to be more creative in my daily tasks. What kind of job are you doing?" Ting asked.

"That kind of work must be very unstable, as it is different every day. I hope you find steady work soon. I am an administrator at an English school downtown now," DanDan mentioned.

"Oh, I didn't know your English was that developed," Ting replied.

"It's even better than the English of the teachers there," DanDan smirked.

"Well, that's good. Actually, my manager sent me this envelope in the mail," Ting said, excitedly, while reaching into her purse.

Harry stumbled out of the bathroom shouting for the other guests in the suite to raise their glasses for a toast. He was dirty, bloody, and reeked of liquor. His long hair was wiry and stuck to his reddened face. Ting's friends hardly understood any English but applauded anyway as Harry excitedly stuttered through a lengthy and incoherent speech. A few of the guests sipped from their glasses as Harry finished his flask and tossed it against one of the walls. The container bounced from the glossy wallpaper, onto the bed and down to the carpeted floors. Ting walked over to Harry once all eyes had veered away from him. She held his hand and intentionally knocked his thigh, asking him what the hard object in his pocket was. Harry mentioned that it was probably a flask and carried on, though Ting persisted in asking him to check his pocket. When he reached into the cargo pocket and removed the soft, black velvet box, he stared at it in a state of confusion.

"Open the box," Ting eagerly commanded.

As Harry slowly opened the box, Ting produced a surprised wail, employing this tactic to capture the attention of all the other guests in the room. She mainly wanted to grab the attention of DanDan. By the time that DanDan realized that Harry had opened a box containing an engagement ring, Ting was already shouting in agreement. DanDan's eyes widened, and an envious look overcame her face. Her eyebrows folded as she wrinkled her face in anger and frantic embarrassment. She was furious that Ting would be getting married before her, again considering that she was the older of the two. DanDan couldn't believe that Ting was working in an office and that she would now be marrying a white man. Ting had found the perfect opportunity to expedite a proposal, while arrogantly putting her seemingly extravagant new lifestyle on display. Harry was one sip away from convulsing and had not noticed what was inside of the box at all. There was only a split second between the opening of the box and Ting's ravaging agreement. She continued to shout "Yes! Yes! Yes!" into his face. Harry felt as though he was nearing a rather severe seizure. He faded out of consciousness while the absurd, passive-aggressive feud between Ting and DanDan continued. Ting had essentially tricked him into proposing to her, but the purpose of her scheme was mainly to establish a higher social status among DanDan and her friends. The night continued as a jealous and bitter DanDan drank to severe drunkenness and a corpse-like Harry barely sustained life.

The two awoke back at Ting's home. Ting was woozy again but stood and walked to the kitchen to see if her grandparents were awake. Harry continued to slumber in his private room. The couple was already feasting on a disgustingly thick porridge and listening to a new announcer on the radio. They excitedly greeted Ting and poured a bowl of cold slop for her to consume. They asked her how her get-together with her friends was the night before. Ting answered briefly and nervously neglected to include any critical details regarding her engagement. She ate the porridge while gauging the mood of her grandparents. Ting thought again about breaking the news that she and Harry were now engaged. However, she knew that the announcement would be a half-truth since

Harry was completely unaware of having become engaged in the first place. They had enjoyed their time with Harry two nights earlier and considered him to be a gentle giant. Their opinion of foreigners had changed as they now viewed them as humorous, harmless drunks. They knew that Ting and Harry would work well together and become stable business partners.

Ting noticed an apparent leniency in them and felt that this was the right opportunity to make her announcement.

"Grandma, I need to tell you something. I wanted to tell you two days ago, but I was afraid that you would not approve," she solemnly stated.

"Oh, child, we have come to terms with your parents' passing. We forgive you. It is no longer your fault," the old woman replied.

Ting uncomfortably exhaled and continued with her original intention to tell them of the engagement.

"Ok, thank you. What do you think of Harry?" she asked.

"He's a funny man!" shouted the grandfather, "These foreign trolls never cease to amaze me!"

"He is very crazy and fun," replied the grandmother, "and he is handsome, indeed."

"Yes, he's very handsome. I'm glad you like him. Would you be upset if I told you that we are dating now?" Ting asked.

"What?!" shouted the old man.

"Impossible!" cried the old woman.

"But you said-"

"Enough of this nonsense!"

"You are dating this villainous, white monster?! How could you even consider such a thing?" asked the grandmother.

"It is forbidden! He is not Chinese! How could the two of you ever communicate? How could he ever support you and raise a family with you?" asked the grandfather.

"The white men only want to ravish the bodies of us Chinese women, but they do not understand family. They only know divorce!" shouted the old lady.

"This is Zhejiang province. You cannot marry outside of our province, let alone marry one of those demonic ghouls!" shouted the grandfather.

"But, you said you liked him! What's the difference if I marry a Chinese man or a white man?" asked Ting, frantically.

"Marry him?! Are you completely out of your mind?" screeched the grandfather, expelling the wretched porridge and covering the kitchen table with blobs of the white goo.

"Ting, my dear child, you have become completely blind. We cannot marry with these grotesque, hairy fools. Imagine what the kids would look like! They would not be white, and they would not be Chinese! They would be hybrid monsters!"

Ting's grandfather began to choke on the porridge as he quivered in extreme shock. He coughed to clear his windpipe, but this was no easy task for the old man. He continued barking at an increasingly elevated volume as his wife began to beat his back with a broomstick to assist him in clearing his throat's passageway. Ting grew furious at their ignorance and immediate disapproval. She stood from her seat and shouted at her grandparents, an act that was considered incredibly insulting and volatile.

"Mao damn you, you ignorant fools!"

Ting's grandmother's eyes expanded, holding back tears as she continued to beat her husband with the broomstick.

"I'm pregnant!" she shouted, as tears streamed down her face, "and you'll both be dead soon anyway!"

Ting grabbed her purse and ran through the front door to escape the house. She could hear her grandfather behind her, gasping and choking. He continued trying to squeeze violent screams through his smothered throat. Ting vowed to never return to Huangyan after the harsh verbal lashing that she had just received. She ran into the street and looked up at the cloudy sky. The city was still enveloped in the metallic fog. She followed the main county road and ran towards downtown Huangyan, hoping to find a nice restaurant to relax in. She wanted to gather her thoughts and return to Shanghai as soon as possible.

CHAPTER FOURTEEN

While Ting had already made it to the small downtown center of Huangyan, Harry was just waking up back at the Lu household. He awoke with his body devastated after another night of drinking. He stepped out of his room and walked into the kitchen. Ting's grandfather was finally overcoming his coughing fit. They froze, motionless, and watched as Harry walked to the cabinet to pour himself a glass of liquor. Their eyes flung open and the old man's face began to tremble in a fury. Within ten seconds, the grandfather had released an angered screech that was heard throughout the neighborhood. The old woman began to beat Harry over the head with the broomstick, clutching it in both hands with a degree of ferocity that caused splinters to enter her old, wrinkled fingers. Harry was caught off-guard by this violent attack. He looked for Ting in a panicked frenzy but soon realized that she was not in the house. Harry's head was being ruthlessly battered by this wicked, old woman, while the grandfather shouted and threw cups of water at Harry's body. He ran through the front door, tripping on the doorstep and collapsing onto the cold, moist concrete in front of the building. He ran away, stopping after about three minutes. He entered the convenience store nearby and picked up a liter of three-penis wine. His reality had been turned upside down, and he was unaware of why the grandparents had reacted so harshly to him removing a glass from the cabinet. The last thing he remembered was nausea within his stomach in the hotel room the night before. He headed towards the city center, walking along the county road so that he would not lose his way.

He could hardly walk and repeatedly stopped to rest along the dusty road. Harry sat and watched the occasional driver speed by him. Most of them nearly crashed after locking eyes with the unidentifiable, foreign creature. He thought of his brothers. He thought of each of them living in their happy, suburban homes with their wives and beautiful little children. He wondered why it couldn't have been him. Harry wondered why out of a family of six boys, he was the only one of the brothers unable to set up a stable home base. Then he thought of his ex-wife. She was probably happier without him, living with another man and planning on someday having a family. Her new lover would certainly be able to provide her with everything she had ever wanted. She would finally have a home, children, and a stable relationship. Harry thought that she was certainly better off without him. He thought back to the days they used to spend together at the park, people-watching and picnicking. Harry would probably never experience joy like that again. Her silky, fair skin was as smooth as a ripe Georgia peach, but he would never be able to feel anything like it again. Instead, his days were being wasted groping the old, hideous street walkers of Hooker Street, with their milky skin and appalling stench.

Harry nearly collapsed on the side of the road in admittance of his complete and utter failures. His visa was about to expire as well, leaving him illegally stranded in this wild land. He hadn't the money to leave the country, let alone exit and reenter. He continued to sit in contemplation.

Harry thought he had hit rock bottom when he arrived in China and resumed his debilitating alcoholism. Rock bottom got deeper for him when he began frequenting Hooker Street, waking up on the floor every morning and hitting the bottle immediately. Harry would spontaneously vomit and tremble violently while lying on the floor of his apartment almost every morning. He fell even deeper into despair and was being kicked out of several brothels night after night. When Harry thought he was experiencing a heart attack in the hotel room with Ting's friends, he nearly called it quits. But now, lying on this wet, gray road, he thought it would be impossible for things to get worse.

His friend Markham was still back in Shanghai enjoying every second of that lifestyle, but deep down, Harry wanted to change. He thought that there was still hope and he slowly pulled himself up from the wet concrete road. Harry sat, perched atop a road barrier, in a complete trance. If he were still able to regain Ting's trust, perhaps she would be able to reform him. Maybe if right now, at this very moment, she took him under her wing, he would make it. After all, Harry had gotten himself into this drunken mess. He had fallen so far down the rabbit hole that nothing in his life seemed to be worth fighting for. Harry could get himself back out, though, he thought. Harry considered several ways to win Ting back so that he could lean on her for support. He sat in deep thought, as it began to drizzle in Huangyan.

Meanwhile, Ting was clinging to her purse as she sat in an old tea shop. The shop was an authentic Zhejiang province landmark, filled with hand-crafted wooden furniture and a variety of teas from rural areas within the region. Ting didn't notice the decorations. She was fed up with these small-town peasants, and she was fed up with Harry. She hated the way he was intoxicated every day, leaving her to weave her web around his inconvenient flaws. Harry was incoherent enough for her to gain near-complete control over him, but this impeded the speed at which she could act as his puppeteer. Surely, she could find another one of these foreigners as quickly as she had found Harry. After all, she had only been in Shanghai for a short time before meeting him. She regretted giving herself to him so soon. DanDan was a nonentity, and there was no purpose in trying to impress her, she thought. Even her friend Hua back in Shanghai was now below Ting. She had acquired a foreign lover much faster than Hua ever could, not to mention Ting was moving up in the corporate world. This was something that Hua could never even come close to achieving.

Ting thought about the baby that Harry had hastily impregnated her with. She was unable to understand how she could have gotten pregnant from just a one night stand. She knew something was wrong after she started experiencing morning sickness, but her fears were confirmed once she received the results of a home pregnancy test. There was no chance that Harry would be a contributing father in his current state. She thought about aborting the child. This was a common act in a country that conducted over 13 million abortions per year. An estimated 10 million additional procedures were expected to have gone unreported. Birth control was available to citizens, but they were simply uneducated on its use and purpose. Ting considered the fact that if she and Harry didn't marry, she would be unable to procure an identity card for the infant. This would prevent the child from ever registering as a Chinese citizen, attending school, opening an official business, and being legitimately employed. The child would be left to find employment as a laborer, slaving away for an entire lifetime while praying for death. These restrictive laws were initially put in place by the government's hierarchy to prevent premarital sexual relations and the onslaught of bastard children that would inevitably result. The regime found this easy. Fabricating hasty laws was pleasantly indirect in comparison to creating tension within communities by offering sexual education courses in public schools. Ting decided that she would likely abort the child, though she would *certainly* abort it if it were a girl. She wouldn't, however, be allowed to know the sex of the baby through an ultrasound screening. This information was illegal to give to expecting mothers in China, due to statistics that showed increased abortion rates for female fetuses. Ting decided that if she sensed she was pregnant with a girl, she would terminate the pregnancy and if anything went wrong, she could always leave the infant girl in the park for some left-behind, elderly woman to find. Additionally, she could always just dump the baby into a garbage can and forget all about it. If her unpleasant acts were unknown to her friends and family, it would be as though they had never occurred in the first place.

Harry had made it to Huangyan's downtown district and began to look for Ting, calling her several times only to reach her voicemail repeatedly. He had concluded that the only way for him to resurrect his failing life was to secure Ting's assistance for the rest of his days. Harry would do this by proposing to her. He didn't have a ring, but quickly found a jewelry store and purchased the least expensive stainless-steel wedding band that they had on sale. Harry quickly jotted down some notes on a torn and liquor-soaked napkin so that he could plan the proposal. He would tell her that she was the best thing that had ever happened to him, that they could build a perfect life together, and that he would sober up and love her every day. Harry thought that she would agree right away, considering how quickly the girl had clung to him when they first met. He called her once more, and she picked up, hesitantly giving him the location of the tea store.

On his way to the store, Harry was overcome with nervousness at the thought of having to propose again for the first time since asking his ex-wife to marry him. He went into a large department store and selected the first liquor bottle he could locate. Bottles of world-renowned liquors surrounded the more traditional, Chinese spirits, but they were mostly counterfeit and hastily brewed from the urine of various homeless dogs. The clerk quickly handed him an exceptional and trusted bottle of deer antler wine. Harry poured the entire bottle down his throat before starting on his way to meet Ting. He began to think of every possible way that the proposal could play out, and he was confident that everything would go well for him. Harry continued walking toward the tea shop, planning his words as carefully as he could while fighting back the effects of the antler wine. When he saw Ting, he fell in love with her all over again. He would vow to stop drinking from this day forward if only he could be with her and spend the rest of his life with her. She was half his age and beautiful, he thought. She would certainly make a great wife and keep him in line well enough for him to stay sober and healthy.

Harry walked into the tea shop and found Ting sitting, in contemplation, next to the store window. In his mind, he had walked in charmingly, but Ting instantly noticed that he was drunk again. She was preparing to gather her things and leave when Harry stumbled over to her. He crashed into a young couple's table and knocked their teapot to the ground. Ting stood up and brushed Harry away. She finally decided that there was no chance for her to salvage this hideous man. Harry tried to comfort her, but she pushed him away to get by. He tripped backward and came crashing down onto the table of another unsuspecting couple. Hot green teas spilled onto his face, burning and scarring his rugged chin. Ting ran out of the shop, and Harry chased after her, scrambling for the steel ring he had purchased. She was walking down the street away from the shop at a brisk pace, trying to avoid Harry and end her relationship with him once and for all.

Harry was on a direct path towards Ting when a street vendor obstructed his view and blocked Harry from passing.

"Hey man, get the fuck out of my way, you damn idiot!" Harry shouted.

The vendor had been set up outside of the tea shop, with multiple wooden barrels of tea leaves set up on display.

Recently, a warning had been released by the U.S. Embassy, cautioning Americans in China that a recent street-tea scam had been ramping up in China. Many tea vendors would attract people to their green tea stands, putting their highest quality products on display. Visitors, and often tourists, would gravitate toward the enticing displays and smell several varieties of teas. They would walk away from the stand, unknowingly having sniffed sedative-based inhalants that would quickly leave them feeling woozy. They would often continue down the street, meandering in wild patterns until one of the tea stand's employees could discretely kidnap them. The organs of the tourists would then be harvested and sold on the Chinese black market for thousands of *yuan*. The visitors would later wake up bleeding in a cold, dark alley. The vendor remained in front of Harry as he tried to catch up to Ting, holding various teas up to his face. The persistent crook shouted a variety of prices for each leaf strain and continued to shove the dried samples into the face of this bearded brute. Harry unwillingly inhaled the scent of the leaves before pushing the vendor aside and tossing him into a pile of garbage that laid beside the road.

Harry instantly became dizzy, but he continued walking on the sidewalk to find Ting. She was about 100 meters in front of him as he stumbled after her, shouting her name and clutching the ring between his fingers. Ting walked without looking back. Harry attempted to run but was quickly hit by a motorized rickshaw on the street. The driver continued, speeding off past Harry's body as Harry slowly stood. He began after Ting again, finally catching up to her. He panted heavily as he tried to overcome both his drunkenness and his dizziness. Harry neared Ting, before stopping and leaning against a street lamp.

"What the fuck was in that tea?!" he shouted under his breath.

"What? Go away," replied Ting.

"Ting… Ting, I love you."

"Love me? Really?" she replied.

"I love you."

"No. No, it's too late."

"Ting, please, I need you."

Ting turned and quickly began to walk away. Harry chased after her once more, stubbing his toe on a rusted metal pole protruding from the edge of the sidewalk.

"Ting, will you marry me?!" he shouted, leaning against a metallic-red fire hydrant.

"Marry *you*?! Hah! What? Hah!" Ting shouted as she rolled her eyes and straightened her purse strap on her shoulder, "You have no job, you have no house, no car, and you have no money."

"But-"

"Why would I marry *you*!?" she shouted as she began to laugh.

Ting turned and rapidly departed from Harry's vicinity as he slouched down onto the edge of the sidewalk. Harry quickly grew dizzier as the effects of the tea combined with the deer antler wine. He collapsed onto the street, and his face landed directly atop a puddle of mud and fish-water. This was a horrendous fluid that was often poured into the street after being used to clean the inside of fish caught from the QianTang River. The river was, by far, the vilest of the earth's natural streams. As he fell, his head collided with a bulging sewer grate and had begun to leak blood. He rolled over slowly and with great struggle. Harry slowly reached for the ring he had purchased for Ting. He held it in front of his face. His breathing slowed as the rest of his body adjusted, falling into place on the dirt-ridden street. Harry looked at the ring and thought of his ex-wife, he thought of the happy marriages his brothers were lucky enough to be a part of, and he thought of Ting. He wished it would have worked out with Ting, but he felt that she was indeed gone for good. Harry stared at the ring, motionless and without blinking for even a moment. He stared at it as a faint, weak smile overcame his grimy face. The toxins settled further into his bloodstream and mixed with his thin blood. His head continued to ooze the bright red velvet. Harry smiled, thinking of Ting, as he took his last breath. The ring rolled out of his hand and danced between the bars of the sewer grate before falling inside. He exhaled and laid, completely motionless, on the street as a crowd slowly began to surround him.

CHAPTER FIFTEEN

Ting looked up at the Huangyan sky for the last time. She was standing at the airport, ready to leave the desolate and miserable town. She vowed to never return, to leave these lowly laborers to their own devices. Without a supportive family and without any sort of potential husband, what was left for her here? Ting stepped into the airport and checked her bags. Behind her, a group of farmers was preparing their cardboard boxes, filled with regional delicacies, for shipment. She had developed an intense disgust for these uneducated and hopeless people. The soiled peasants glanced at Ting, who was dressed in a beautiful, red wool jacket. They smiled in admiration as she turned her head toward the front desk clerk.

Ting reached into her purse and pulled out the yellow envelope that her manager had sent her via certified mail just days before. Her recent successes and promotions at the Double Happy Good Smoke headquarters had not only earned her a larger paycheck but a certain amount of *guanxi* that connected her throughout the world. International corporate executives could certainly use her developed skills. Her manager immediately took notice of her quick hands typing in the office, her ability to maneuver the complex multi-lateral system of paperwork, and her ability to complete her assignments in a rather timely manner. She was targeted for the fast-route promotion ladder from day one. Ting slowly unfolded the envelope and pried it open at the torn edge. The envelope contained a passport and a single, one-way ticket, redeemable as an airline credit to be used at any given time. In the passport, she located the work visa stamped into page 42, valid for one year. Ting handed both documents to the clerk and loaded her small luggage case onto the conveyor belt. She received her stamped receipt and was pointed in the direction of the boarding gate. She looked outside through the giant, glass windows at the haze for the last time. Ting then looked down at her ticket.

She needed to make it to gate G7 to board. Her eyes scanned the rest of the boarding pass as she gazed, in a dream-like state, at the bold text that danced on the ticket and fluttered through her mind:

"Destination: New York (JFK)."

TO BE CONTINUED...